SPECIAL MESSAGE TO READERS

THE ULVERSCROFT FOUNDATION
(registered UK charity number 264873)

was established in 1972 to provide funds for research, diagnosis and treatment of eye diseases. Examples of major projects funded by the Ulverscroft Foundation are:

- The Children's Eye Unit at Moorfields Eye Hospital, London
- The Ulverscroft Children's Eye Unit at Great Ormond Street Hospital for Sick Children
- Funding research into eye diseases and treatment at the Department of Ophthalmology, University of Leicester
- The Ulverscroft Vision Research Group, Institute of Child Health
- Twin operating theatres at the Western Ophthalmic Hospital, London
- The Chair of Ophthalmology at the Royal Australian College of Ophthalmologists

You can help further the work of the Foundation by making a donation or leaving a legacy. Every contribution is gratefully received. If you would like to help support the Foundation or require further information, please contact:

THE CIRCUS OF FEAR

The circus folk had been Kat's family after her parents died during a dangerous stunt in the ring. Her relationship with trapeze artist Jake had ended over her fear of him taking risks. Now she was back after ten years in the outside world, fleeing her own drama — but why was everyone so unwelcoming? Where was her best friend, Delilah — and who was the sinister new ringmaster?

First published in Great Britain in 2023 by
D.C. Thomson & Co. Ltd.
Dundee

First Linford Edition
published 2024
by arrangement with
the author and
D.C. Thomson & Co. Ltd.
Dundee

A catalogue record for this book is available from the British Library.

ISBN 978–1–4448–5424–4

Published by
Ulverscroft Limited
Anstey, Leicestershire

Printed and bound in Great Britain by
TJ Books Ltd., Padstow, Cornwall

This book is printed on acid-free paper

JACQUI COOPER

THE CIRCUS OF FEAR

Complete and Unabridged

LINFORD
Leicester

1

As Katelyn Turner stepped off the bus, the loud beat of music and the sweet scent of popcorn reached her on the breeze, drawing her attention to the huge red-and-white striped tent standing on a hill in a field opposite.

She checked her phone. Still no message from her friend Delilah.

'We're going to the circus,' said a little boy who had been on the same bus.

His excitement was palpable. Kat stuffed her phone back into her pocket and smiled.

'Me too.'

A clown on six-foot-high stilts was playing to the stream of people flocking towards the big top.

'Look!' yelled the boy. 'A clown. A real clown. We have to hurry.' He grabbed his mum's hand.

'He's so excited,' the woman told Kat, allowing herself to be dragged along.

'He's barely spoken about anything else for weeks.'

'I hear it's a great show.' Kat swung her rucksack onto her back.

Crossing the road together, the three went through the gate into the field. With a great show of flailing arms and almost-but-not-quite tripping over his huge shoes, the towering clown made a beeline straight for them.

Kat recognised him immediately. Noodle. He and his wife Nellie, also a clown, had been kind to her when her parents died. Luckily for her, Noodle was too focused on the child to pay the adults any attention. Even so, Kat allowed her long, dark hair to swing casually in front of her face, deciding she'd rather meet Delilah first to find out what — if anything — her friend had told people about what had prompted this visit after almost ten years away.

'Hi. I'm Noodle. What's your name?' The clown waggled his fingers and the little boy, suddenly shy, pressed closer to his mother.

'S . . . Sam.'

'Watch me, Sam!' Noodle showed him first one empty palm, then the other. A second later a fully inflated balloon tied to a string appeared from nowhere. He bowed from the waist and offered it to Sam with a flourish.

Sam stretched out his hand to take it.

'Mum, did you see that? Did you see what he did?' he asked Kat, eyes shining.

'Amazing,' said his mum.

'Incredible,' said Kat. She had seen the trick a thousand times over the years but the thrill in each child's eyes never grew old.

'Tickets are selling fast,' said Noodle before tripping and flailing his way to the next child.

'That was brilliant,' said Sam's mum. 'How did he do that?'

'Magic.' Kat checked her phone. No message.

'Expecting a call?'

'I was supposed to meet a friend.' Kat was growing worried. When they'd last spoken, Delilah had been really enthusiastic about Kat's visit. Had she changed her mind?

Sam's mum eyed Kat's rucksack and rolled-up sleeping bag, her gaze also taking in her biker boots, jeans and well-worn leather jacket. Kat could guess what she was thinking. *Aren't you a little old to be running away with the circus?*

And yes, at twenty-eight she probably was.

Was this even a good idea? She'd been gone so long. And with her face plastered all over the news, would anyone but Delilah even want her here?

Knowing she had no other options, she continued up the grassy slope towards the big top.

On the right of the huge tent, a line of glossy black horses were being groomed in the sunshine. It was impossible not to admire their sleek beauty. Further back was a cluster of trucks and wagons with the Circus Mara logo. The performers' caravans would be behind the big top, offering some privacy to those for whom the circus was home.

Kat was pleased to see that both the horses and wagons looked in tip-top condition. It seemed Circus Mara was flourishing under Jake's management.

Jake. It was as if just thinking his name had somehow conjured him up as she watched a tall, dark-haired man striding towards the wagons. Seven years had passed since she'd last seen him but she'd know that loose, rangy walk anywhere.

'Are you OK?' asked Sam's mum, glancing over to see what had caught her attention. 'Oooh. Nice. Is that your friend?'

'No,' said Kat quickly. She and Jake hadn't been friends in a long time.

'Muuum,' pleaded Sam. 'We'll miss it.'

'Sorry. We'd better get in the queue.'

Kat made a decision. If she couldn't get hold of Delilah, she may as well watch the show.

'Can you keep me a place while I ring my friend?'

'Sure. Come on, Sam.'

* * *

According to the flashing red neon countdown timer writing and rewriting itself above the box office, the show was due to start in under ten minutes. Kat made a quick call but didn't let it ring for long — the last thing Delilah needed this close to a performance was a distraction.

The real purpose of the call was to give her a few minutes to bring order to her rattled thoughts. How could the mere sight of Jake have this effect on her, even after all this time?

Waiting for her racing pulse to return to normal, she tried to convince herself that actually it was a good thing she had seen him like this, from a distance. This way she'd be over the initial reaction when they inevitably bumped into each other later.

Yes. It was a good thing. Once she could breathe.

Jake climbed into the cab of one of the trucks and only then, when he was out of sight, did she begin to feel normal.

A blur of movement caught her eye

and what she saw made her gasp. One of the horses had broken free from his tether and, glossy head held high, was trotting purposefully towards the ticket queue and the freedom of the open field beyond.

The man chasing him, waving his arms and yelling, did nothing to encourage the animal to stop. People in his path jumped aside, frantically pulling children out of the way.

This was a circus animal, used to noise and people. Logic told Kat that the chances of him panicking were minimal, but she couldn't say the same for the crowd. Someone — human or animal — was going to get hurt.

Years ago a woman called Phaedra had been in charge of the Circus Mara horses. As a teenager, Kat had often helped, both with mucking out and in the ring. Knowing she might be just about to make a monumental fool of herself, she stepped into the horse's path. Her pulse hammered as the powerful animal bore down on her.

Waiting until she saw his ears prick forward, showing that he had seen her, she gave a subtle hand signal that her memory had dredged up from the past. To her immense relief, the well-trained horse pivoted on his front foot and trotted back up the hill, where, blowing and snorting, he allowed himself to be caught.

The whole thing took seconds. As far as Kat could tell, no one even noticed what she'd done.

'Are you all right?' Sam's mum beckoned her over. 'You could have been killed!'

Noodle sprinted up the hill as fast as his stilts and oversized shoes would allow.

'Watch me!' He called his catchphrase and everyone did.

'All part of the show, folks,' he said, chuckling breathlessly. 'More thrills inside. Hurry, hurry.'

He shot Kat a curious glance and once more she swiftly turned away, taking her place with Sam and his mum in the queue.

Noodle let out a piercing whistle. Seconds later Kat heard a raucous squawk overhead and a chorus of yells from the crowd as a large scarlet, blue and yellow bird skimmed over their heads, low enough to ruffle their hair.

Captain! The name came to her in a flash. Kat was delighted the old macaw was still around.

'Watch me!' shrieked Captain and dived for Noodle's hat. While the clown yelled and pretended to fend him off, the bird continued to swoop and cackle and the tense crowd erupted in laughter. As damage control, it was sheer perfection.

Kat spotted Phaedra, older now but still stunning in full stage make-up and a white tuxedo, hurrying over to check her runaway horse. Jake, too, had jumped down from the wagon and was making his way to the horse line, his face like thunder. His route would take him directly past Kat. Swiftly turning her back, she grinned at Sam's mum.

'It's all go, isn't it!'

‘I know!’ The other woman fanned herself with her hand. ‘I’m already in a state and the show hasn’t even started!’

Minutes later, Kat had reached the walk-through wagon that served as a box office. Inside, hidden from Jake’s view, she breathed a sigh of relief. Luckily she didn’t recognise the man selling tickets.

‘Is Delilah in tonight’s show?’ she asked, handing over her money.

‘How should I know?’

Kat blinked.

‘There’s a queue, lady.’ He jerked his head, indicating she should move on.

* * *

First a loose horse, now rudeness to a paying customer? Kat was still processing this when she entered the big top, and so was completely unprepared for the fierce blast of nostalgia that hit with the scent of flattened grass and sawdust.

In an instant she was nine years old again, lying on her back on these very benches, watching her parents climb up to the glittering stars on the roof of the tent, where they swung as casually on the trapeze as other parents would on a garden swing. Kat looked up, imagining them waving at her . . .

'Excuse me.'

She realised she was blocking the entrance.

'Over here,' called Sam's mum. 'Come and sit with us. You didn't find your friend?'

'Not yet.'

Kat only just had time to sit down and tuck her rucksack by her feet before the lights dimmed and the familiar circus theme tune — *Entry Of The Gladiators* — began to boom out.

A spotlight shone on the centre of the ring, revealing a traditional ringmaster in a scarlet coat, white jodhpurs and boots — and just like that, the show was underway.

Kat had seen thousands of circus performances but it was hard not to get caught up in the sheer showmanship, professionalism and yes, magic, as one spectacular act followed another.

Noodle and Nellie filled buckets with water and threw them into the crowd, who shrieked in horror then laughed in relief when the water miraculously turned to tissue paper. Acrobats and jugglers made what should have been impossible look easy. The six gorgeous black liberty horses — that is, with no lead reins or riders — trotted and turned in sync guided only by Phaedra's voice, or her long, flexible stick with which she signalled where they should go next without actually touching them. The audience, mainly families, lapped it up.

Kat was equally entranced. Until . . .

'Ladies and gentlemen,' boomed the ringmaster, thumping his silver topped cane for silence. 'Boys and girls. For your delectation. For your delight. Hoooold onto your seats and hold your breath.

'Pray sileeence for . . .' a drumroll sounded '. . . The Wheel of Death!'

Kat felt the colour drain from her face. Delilah hadn't mentioned this was part of the show. But knowing how Kat felt about the act, she wouldn't.

Kat wasn't ready for it. Panicked, she grabbed her bag, ready to escape. But the lights went down, plunging the tent into darkness, leaving her stuck.

Shadowy figures moved about in near darkness as the wheel was rapidly assembled. Two human skeletons danced in behind it and there was a collective gasp from the audience until they realised they were men in close-fitting black outfits printed with glowing neon bones and grinning skulls.

'Ladies and gentlemen,' went on the ringmaster, 'I give you Marty Allen and Jake Romero!'

Jake? No. No. Blood thundered in Kat's ears.

Jake — the man she had once loved more than life itself — was about to take part in the act that had killed both her parents?

2

With the men costumed and masked, Kat had no way of knowing which one was Jake, meaning she had to divide her worry equally between them.

As the music started up and the lights began strobing, all she could do was pray.

Kat knew that in the circus, danger was often a carefully crafted illusion. But she also knew better than most that accidents could and did happen. And when they did, they could be terrible.

The Wheel of Death was notorious, respected and feared by circus performers the world over.

The wheel itself was a monstrous contraption. Two long arms like the hands of a giant clock were attached to a tall, upright metal support. At the end of each arm was a giant hamster wheel, big enough to fit a man inside and allow him to move freely. As the arms rotated, moving the wheels, the wheels too, spun independently. At the height of each revolution the top wheel was thirty feet off the ground, the bottom one skimming the sawdust.

Kat's mouth was dry as the two cavorting skeletons set the arms spinning. When one wheel reached ground level the first man stepped inside as casually as if he was getting on a bus. As he was lifted to the roof of the tent the other wheel descended and the second man did the same.

Round and round they went, each running inside their wheel, their momentum increasing the speed. The music grew louder. The wheels spun faster. The lights danced. Excitement built in the audience as the men began to jump and tumble inside the wheels. Then a gasp went up as, on the upsweep, they stepped out of their wheel and continued to run and jump and dance on the outside rim — a seemingly impossible task and fraught with danger as the two arms continued to revolve and the two wheels continued to spin.

Any mis-step could mean a broken leg. Or neck. Or worse. And the crowd lapped it up.

Unable to tear her gaze away, Kat watched. Only when the final cheer went up could she unclench both jaw and fists. The men had their feet firmly on the ground and they ripped their masks off as they took their bows. Jake's dark hair was plastered to his forehead but he looked as pleased with himself as only a man who had just cheated death could.

This stupid, casual, grinning addiction to danger was one of the reasons Kat had finally abandoned circus life — and Jake. He had begged and pleaded and explained over and over that the danger was controlled, that the risks he took were exaggerated for effect. But how could she believe him when her parents had died taking those exact same risks?

Before their deaths, Kat never questioned anything about her upbringing or way of life. Afterwards she'd questioned everything. Things she had always accepted as normal were suddenly exposed as anything but.

Jake had tried to see things her way. But the circus was his life, and she knew he could never fully understand the intense feeling of dread that had taken root inside her, spreading inexorably until it threatened to consume her.

She'd known she couldn't continue to live this way. Just as, deep down, she'd known Jake couldn't live any other way.

Already the wheel was being dismantled and stowed as the ringmaster announced the interval. The lights came on and the blinking audience turned their attention to the popcorn sellers who had appeared like genies from a lamp.

Kat grabbed her rucksack and with a murmur to Sam and his mum, slipped out of the tent. She'd find Delilah and hopefully wait out the second half of the show in her caravan. Delilah's current act was trapeze; watching one death-defying act was more than enough for one day.

* * *

The Delectable Delilah's candy pink caravan was easy to spot. With a retro Fifties look it was smaller than the surrounding caravans and trailers but the lurid — Del would say vibrant — colour made Kat smile. She knocked softly on the door.

'Delilah? It's me.'

Phaedra, walking past leading two of her horses, shot Kat a glance but didn't stop.

'Delilah?' Kat knocked again, more urgently.

The door slammed open abruptly. A man Kat had never seen before glared down at her.

'Sorry. I'm looking for Delilah,' she said.

'You're not allowed back here. Performers only.'

'I'm a friend. She's expecting me.'

'Yeah, right.' He reached to close the door.

Kat was willing to bet there was only one bright pink caravan in the field. Besides, there was a larger than life image of Delilah in her trademark candy-pink body stocking on the side.

'She's expecting me,' she said again.

'She's not here.'

He yanked at the door but Kat swung her rucksack forward to block it.

'Wait! Can you at least tell me where she is?'

He kicked the rucksack out of the way and jumped down onto the grass with a speed and lightness that caught her by surprise. He was a big man and smelled none too fresh. Kat hated herself for taking a step back.

'What did I just tell you?' he growled.

'What's going on?'

The angry male voice behind her made Kat spin and she came face to face with . . . Jake?

Phaedra was hovering anxiously behind him, and Kat guessed the horse trainer had recognised her and gone to fetch him.

The years had been good to him. He had that kind of raw, masculine appeal that made women of all ages steal second and third glances just to check he was real; thick, dark hair, strong jaw, and those striking green eyes.

Kat's nostrils flared, scenting sawdust, and horse, and fresh male sweat from his recent exertions.

Presumably Phaedra had caught him on his way back to his caravan to change; he'd removed the top half of his skeleton outfit, revealing a well-defined chest dusted with black hair, and a belly that looked as hard and ridged as a washboard. Not many men could carry off skeleton tights but Jake achieved it with ease. Kat kept her gaze high.

Jake did not look pleased to see her. In fact, he looked downright furious.

'What are you doing here?' he demanded.

'Nice to see you too, Jake.'

She hadn't meant the flippancy but his open hostility was a shock. Yes, they had parted on bad terms but that was ten years ago. She'd moved on in that time. Surely he had too.

'I've come to see Delilah,' Kat said.

'But muggins here won't tell me where she is.'

'She left,' said Jake.

Noodle and Nellie, still in their clown outfits, joined Phaedra. Nellie smiled broadly until Noodle elbowed her and the smile vanished.

In fact, a small crowd of circus performers had begun to gather. And none of them looked any more welcoming than Jake.

Over the past few weeks, as her life had publicly fallen apart, Kat had become well-schooled at hiding her emotions. Now she realised how much she'd been hoping for something more . . . accepting . . . from these, her oldest friends. She refused to reveal just how much their rejection hurt.

'Where did she go?' she asked Jake.

'I told you, she left.'

'I spoke to her yesterday. She invited me here.'

Del had been happy, excited about the visit and with good news of her own to share, apparently.

'Then she must have changed her mind. Sorry, but you'll have to leave.'

'Get rid of her, Romero.' The man from Delilah's caravan found his voice.

'I'm handling this, Finn,' Jake snapped. 'Kat, you have to go. Now.'

Kat hadn't expected her return to be all hearts and flowers, not with the ugly events of her life currently plastered all over the papers. But these people had been her family. Some of them had even helped raise her. She'd expected some reservations, but never this open hostility.

Stupid, stupid tears stung her eyes but she stood her ground. OK, let them think the worst of her. She was getting used to that. But she wasn't leaving until she had spoken to Delilah and made sure she was OK.

A woman hurrying aound the side of the caravan came to an abrupt halt, seeing the small gathering.

'Hey you lot, get a move on. The band's starting!' And then she recognised Kat and her jaw dropped.

'We're coming,' said Jake. Suddenly everyone was moving. 'Just go,' he told Kat. His final words cut her to the quick. 'No one wants you here.'

Kat was still processing the emotion she had seen in the other woman's eyes.

Fear.

* * *

Kat? Jake's mind raced. All those imagined reunions he'd played and replayed in his head over the years, and she had to turn up now, at the worst possible time?

Why? How? This was a nightmare.

He raced to his trailer to change for the next act, then sped back to the big top.

'Is it true Kat's here?' asked Xerxes, the strong man.

'Not for long,' said Jake praying it was true. 'Come on, everyone. Places.'

'Darrius won't like it,' persisted Xerxes. For such a powerful man he was a bag of nerves. 'What if —'

‘I told you,’ said Jake sharply. ‘She’s not staying. Now go. Get ready. That means all of you!’ he called to the small audience that had gathered.

‘Laaaadies and gentlemeeeen, boys and girls . . .’

Jake gritted his teeth as, on the other side of the heavy red velvet curtain, Darrius began his spiel.

How Jake loathed the man.

Luckily Darrius loved the sound of his own voice. The ringmaster joked and played to the audience though Jake could sense his simmering anger over the unexplained delay.

Still, Jake didn’t rush his safety checks. Some of the new men were slapdash. Like the one who should have been minding Phaedra’s horses. Fury filled him at the thought of the damage that might have been done — to a member of the public, the horse, or the circus’s reputation. He tamped the fury down. It was neither the time nor the place.

Darrius made a barbed comment about keeping everyone waiting but only when Jake was sure everything was in order backstage, did he give the nod to the two young women who were eagerly waiting to climb to the roof of the tent. He wasn't one hundred percent convinced their new trapeze act was ready, but with Delilah gone, he had no choice but to give them the chance they'd been begging for. He did insist they wear safety harnesses though, much to their disgust.

Once they were in place, he climbed to a similar platform on the opposite side of the ring. Like most circus performers, he was used to doing more than one act. As he climbed, he wondered if Kat was there in the audience looking up, fearful, afraid.

Hopefully she'd taken his advice and left. But recalling the stubborn set of her jaw, he doubted it.

Poised high above the upturned faces of the audience, he closed his eyes for a second to clear his mind, then he gripped the trapeze bar and sailed out into nothingness.

* * *

After the final act he pulled on a jumper and jeans and went looking for Kat, finding her behind the big top, hugging Nellie. A couple of the other performers looked as if they might want to hug her too but one glance at Jake bearing down on them and they hastily changed their minds.

Kat looked . . . well, not good. Her long, dark hair was lacklustre and the shadows under her eyes spoke of sleepless nights. Her eyes were as deep and blue as ever but darting and watchful. She'd always been slender; now she verged on skinny.

He tried to find some satisfaction that life on the outside hadn't been the idyll she'd expected. Tried and failed because despite all that had passed between them, he had never wished her ill.

Only once in recent years had he asked Delilah about her. She'd told him Kat had a job, a house, and a fiancé. And while the knowledge had pierced him like a knife, he'd been glad she had found happiness and had never asked again.

Darrius was approaching. Swearing under his breath, he hurried to reach Kat and took her arm.

'You have to go,' he said urgently.

'Can't she just stay for a —' said Nellie. Then she too saw Darrius and gave a frightened little moan.

3

Kat looked from Nellie to Jake and back, puzzled.

'What's going on? I don't understand.'

'Jacob?'

She turned and recognised the ringmaster.

'Pray tell, who is this beautiful stranger?'

Kat knew Jake hated being called Jacob. As a child he'd refused to answer when teachers in each new school had called out the register. Now she waited for him to react but to her amazement, all he said was, 'I'm handling this, Darrius.'

'Are you?' The ringmaster looked at Kat and his smile might have been charming, had it reached his glittering silver eyes.

Her skin prickled as instinct warned her to be careful of this man, even as a less primitive part of her brain told her she was being silly.

She gently tested Jake's grip on her arm.

'Yes, Darrius, I am. And in answer to your question, she's no one,' said Jake.

The casual cruelty in his words hit Kat like a slap.

'Now, Jacob,' chided Darrius, his attention still focused on Kat. 'That's not true. She's clearly someone. And she's here. In my circus.'

'Your circus?' asked Kat, surprised.

'Well, not mine, of course,' said Darrius smoothly. 'I just meant that people have made me feel so at home. Isn't that right, everyone?'

Jake was the only one to give any kind of answer.

'She's just visiting. And now she's leaving.'

'Visiting? Who?' asked Darrius.

Jake squeezed Kat's arm. If he was trying to communicate something, she had no idea what.

'Delilah,' she said.

No one spoke.

'Will someone please just tell me where she is?'

The silence was total. The tension palpable. Everyone was looking at the ground. All except Darrius who was looking at Jake, and Jake who was looking at Kat.

'You're here to see Delilah?' asked Darrius.

'I've told her she's not here,' said Jake quickly.

'But where is she?' demanded Kat. 'And why didn't she tell me she was leaving?'

'Isn't it obvious?' said Jake. 'She doesn't want to see you. Why can't you grasp that none of us want you here?'

Oh, she was beginning to grasp that. She looked around at her old friends, none of whom would meet her eye, and wrenched her arm free.

'I'm not leaving.'

'Why?'

The shame was overwhelming and the tears were real.

'Because I have nowhere to go.'

* * *

Everyone dispersed soon after that. Jake led Kat to his caravan.

It was one of the biggest on the site and very well appointed. It had a dishwasher, a washing machine and with the walls designed to extend outwards when parked, a spacious sitting room. Storage was built into every available nook and cranny.

Kat had been born and raised in a caravan — though admittedly not one as grand as this. Travelling was all she had known for much of her life so she took a moment to look around and appreciate the elegant use of space.

Jake let her take it in, saying nothing. Kat wanted to ask if he remembered the converted lorry they'd shared, way back when their worldly possessions had been a clothes rack and a bed. At nineteen, they hadn't even needed the clothes rack.

Jake was watching her closely. Something flickered behind his dark eyes as if he could read her thoughts. Kat looked away first.

'You can stay here tonight,' he said.

'Thanks.' Kat didn't even attempt to hide her relief. The circus was pitched on farm land. She had no way of getting back to town and nowhere to stay once she got there. 'I can bunk on the settee.'

Jake shook his head. 'Take my room.'

'This is fine, honest.'

He pinched the bridge of his nose.

'It's been a long and trying day, Kat. Can you ever just not argue?'

'I'll take the spare room then.' The van was so spacious, it must have more than one bedroom.

'No!' The sharp retort made her jump. 'What I mean is, the . . . er . . . bed isn't made up in there.'

'I have a sleeping bag.' She gestured towards her rucksack. It would be nice to pretend she'd brought the sleeping bag because she didn't want to put Delilah to any trouble but the truth was, she'd been sleeping on friends' sofas for weeks.

Without asking, Jake stood up and poured them both a drink. She took the glass, the smoky scent of whisky bringing a nostalgic reminder of her father.

'I may be ignorant of how the outside world functions but I'm sure school teachers don't tend to live out of rucksacks,' he said.

School teacher? Kat only lasted a year on that course and hadn't even bothered sitting her exams. Delilah hadn't told him of her change of career?

Which maybe wasn't so strange. Circus people and police didn't tend to mix well, with prejudice often rife on both sides. But if they didn't know she was a detective sergeant — let alone a suspended one — then why such hostility towards her?

Jake was waiting and she shrugged.

'What can I say? Sometimes life has its own ideas. Cheers.' She raised her glass.

Jake's mouth twisted into a sudden wry smile, at once so familiar it tugged at something deep inside her. He, too, raised his glass as he sat down.

'Doesn't it just. I'll drink to that.'

For a moment they sat in a silence

that was almost companionable. It was Kat who broke it.

'Where is she, Jake?' she asked quietly, appealing to the Jake behind that smile. The Jake who'd played hide and seek with her and Delilah between the wagons, and cadged candy floss to share with the horses when Phaedra wasn't looking.

For a brief second, that Jake looked back at her and she dared to hope she would finally get an answer. But the curtain came down once more.

'She's gone.'

There was no hesitation, no deliberating about changing his story now they were alone.

'I spoke to her yesterday,' Kat insisted. 'She knew I was coming. People don't just pack up and leave without a word.'

'Don't they?'

She made herself meet his gaze. No way was she going there. Not now.

'I'm worried about her, Jake.'

He swallowed, his Adam's apple bobbing visibly. He was so handsome, even with five o'clock shadow on his strong jaw.

So very different from her fiancé's — ex-fiancé's — blond good looks and surface sophistication. But that was all Nathan had been; surface. Scratch that surface and everything had been fake.

Jake sighed heavily.

'I don't know what more I can tell you. And to be honest, I can't help thinking Delilah would have told you herself if she wanted you to know her plans.'

That at least had a ring of truth.

'She's OK, though?'

'Yes.' Something flickered in his eyes.

Jake had known Delilah as long as she had, loved her as much as she did. Kat had to take his word for it.

He stood up, his drink barely touched.

'I'll leave you to it. I have to do my rounds.'

Her father had done the same every night before bed, checking the animals, checking that everything was locked up or fastened down.

'You kept the name,' blurted Kat.

Circus Mara had been named after her mother, Mara Capelli Turner.

With his back still turned to her, Jake shrugged.

'What can I say? Circus loves tradition.'

And he was gone.

* * *

Jake didn't return to the caravan that night. Kat had no idea where he slept and was too exhausted to worry about it. She simply unrolled her sleeping bag and lay down on his bed.

When she woke next morning she could hear activity outside and felt guilty for oversleeping while the circus came to life. Animals had to be fed, repairs made, advertising, training and rehearsals all to be arranged.

After the briefest of showers she dressed quickly before going outside, her long hair still damp. Families usually ate together in their own caravans, but back in the day single people, or those who didn't want to cook, had gathered at the clown's caravan where Nellie ran a sideline in home-cooked food, serving it in a tent if the weather was bad. Kat was pleased to see the arrangement still stood.

Today the trestle table was set up in the sunshine. Silence fell as she approached and she was sure they had been talking about her. Thankfully yesterday's shock seemed to have worn off and she was mainly greeted with curiosity.

Phaedra shuffled up to allow her to sit.

'Am I right in thinking it was you who stopped Boris yesterday? Noodle says he saw you in the ticket queue.'

'Boris?'

'My runaway.'

Kat nodded.

'Thank you,' said Phaedra sincerely. 'My poor baby could have been seriously hurt.'

'What was he thinking?' asked Kat. 'I mean the guy who let him go.'

'He is a thug,' stated Phaedra, disdainfully. 'A brute. He doesn't know how to think.'

Kat stored that piece of information away. Circus people were like everyone else, with friendships and enemies. But normally there was respect, too. No one knew who they would be working with tomorrow, who would be assembling or dismantling their equipment. There was rarely open hostility like that which Phaedra clearly felt.

Nellie put a plate of bacon and eggs in front of Kat. Suddenly she was starving.

'So.' Nellie poured a coffee and squeezed onto the bench. 'What have you been up to, love?'

Kat was acutely aware that Delilah had seen fit to keep her job a secret. She must have had a reason for that. Besides, she really didn't want to talk about her train wreck of a life.

'This and that.'

'Teaching?'

She shook her head. 'I changed my mind.'

Nellie nodded sagely. 'I always felt that was too sedate for you. Although I suppose you could have taught the kids to juggle.'

'With fire,' said Xerxes, chuckling. 'Remember when your mum caught you with matches, trying to set some tennis balls alight to juggle with them? What age were you? About six? She was so mad.'

Everyone laughed, including Kat.

It was wonderful, sitting in the sunshine, eating good food and catching up with old friends. It was a simple pleasure very much lacking in Kat's life since her fiancé Nathan's arrest and her suspension. She felt disloyal for not mentioning Delilah, but was unwilling to risk spoiling the mood just yet.

'What happened to Kevin?' she asked.

Kevin had been ringmaster in her parents' day.

'He retired. Living in Bournemouth. We'll see him on our last stop at the end of the season.'

'He always liked it there,' said Kat and everyone agreed. She felt a fleeting sadness that one more link to her parents was gone. But at least Kevin had lived to enjoy his retirement.

'And the new guy? Darrius, is it?'

Everyone fell silent.

'He seemed to know how to work the crowd,' said Kat, well aware she was doing the same thing.

'Oh yes,' sneered Noodle. 'He can do that all right. He's not circus, though.'

Kat's ears pricked up.

'No? So how did he —'

'He's an investor.'

Jake seemed able to appear out of nowhere but Kat remembered he always could tread lightly as a cat. She watched him help himself to coffee.

'Why?' she quipped. 'Do you need the money?'

Everyone laughed at her joke. Circuses always needed money.

Jake looked like an unmade bed, his dark hair mussed and rumpled from finger combing, making her wonder where he had slept. With his arrival a certain amount of tension returned to the group.

'It seems Darrius Bell always harboured dreams of working in a circus,' said Jake easily. 'He has more money than sense, so this is his way in. We get a ringmaster who will perform for free, he gets to dress up and boss people around. It's win, win. Ah, there you are at last.'

This last comment was directed to a blond man who was making his way towards them. Kat recognised Delilah's brother and squealed in genuine delight.

'Charlie!'

She leapt up and threw her arms around him.

'If you won't take it from me that Delilah is OK, maybe you'll take it from him,' said Jake.

Charlie returned her hug.

'It's great to see you, Kat. I'm just sorry you've come all this way for nothing. I . . . I can't believe Del did this to you.'

Kat studied him carefully at arm's length.

'Do you know where she is?'

'No, sorry. But I spoke to her yesterday.' He flicked a glance at Jake. 'I . . . I think she just had to get away for a few days.'

'You spoke to her yesterday? And she didn't mention I was coming?'

'No. Sorry.' He licked his lips. 'If I hear from her again I'll definitely ask her to call you.'

Kat looked from him to the others. One or two couldn't meet her eye. Every instinct told her she was missing something, but these were good people who loved Delilah and would never hurt her.

So why was she so sure that every single one of them was lying?

4

Kat helped Nellie clear up after breakfast. Then she wandered the circus, catching up with old friends, helping out wherever she could.

She found a group of kids playing inside the big top. A wooden board lay on the ground with four flexible poles sticking up from it and they were taking it in turns to spin dinner plates on the poles, with varying levels of success.

Kat watched until they noticed her and stopped.

'Shouldn't you be in school?' she asked, wondering when she had turned into such an adult.

'It's a holiday,' one boy informed her guilelessly.

'It's pull down tonight,' said another, more honestly.

Pull down. When the Big Top came down and the circus moved on overnight. Even in Kat's day circus kids had treated pull down like the last day of term, with attendance optional, and the adults had turned a blind eye. After all, the next day they'd start at a brand new school, so why would today's school bother to chase them for a day's absence?

'Do you want a go?' asked a boy of about ten, indicating the plates.

Kat made a face. 'I don't know. It looks hard.'

'It's easy,' the kids insisted. 'Look.' They demonstrated.

'OK. I'll give it a try. Like this?'

She took a plate, set it on top of a pole and started it spinning. The plate went flying and she only just caught it before it smashed.

The children laughed.

'You have to steady it. And spin faster.'

This time she kept the plate spinning though she almost killed herself as she danced around the pole, arms waving frantically, ready to catch it.

'Now try two!'

Kat didn't dare take her eye off the one spinning plate. She held out her hand for another then tried to balance it on the pole. For a brief second both were spinning before the first one fell off followed by the second. Kat dived for both, executing a perfect somersault and landing on her feet, both plates intact in her outstretched hands.

Clicking her heels together, she took a bow, breathless but exhilarated. The children were staring open-mouthed.

'You tricked us,' said one indignantly.

'No, she played you,' said Noodle who had arrived while the show was going on. 'This, boys and girls, is Kat Turnado, best assistant I ever had. Now clear off, all of you, before someone finds you something to do.'

The children ran off.

Noodle was in full make-up even though the show wouldn't start for hours. Kat could count on one hand the times she'd seen him without it.

'You always had a talent for that,' he said.

Most people on a travelling circus were multi-skilled by necessity, and Kat had been no exception. She'd had a talent for lots of things and, growing up, she had been given free rein to develop those that interested her. She'd been blessed with a slim, athletic build, a quick mind and no fear of heights.

Her proud parents had assumed she would follow them onto the trapeze but while Kat loved training with them, she had never really settled on any one skill. Instead, she'd become a jack of all trades, able to clown around with Noodle and Nellie, throw knives with Xerxes or walk a high wire.

Suddenly and sharply, Kat missed those times. Missed them deep in that part of her where she held her parents' memory.

She picked up the plates to tidy them away.

Noodle had been watching her closely.

'So what are your plans now?'

Kat couldn't bring herself to tell her old friend that she honestly had no idea.

'Leave and wait for Delilah to call, I guess.'

'We missed you, you know.'

'But now, suddenly, you all want me gone?'

'Things are complicated.' Noodle looked away.

'Why?' asked Kat. 'I don't understand.'

To Noodle's obvious relief, someone needed his help and he made his excuses and hurried off.

'Don't be such a stranger next time,' he called.

Left alone, Kat pondered his question. What were her plans now?

She couldn't stay in the circus. Without Delilah she didn't have a bed and she could hardly expect to impose on Jake, since he'd made it quite clear that putting her up last night was a one-off.

She had no family and she'd probably overstayed her welcome with the few friends she had left.

Of course she had a key to Nathan's house, but if the press were still camped outside hustling for an interview, then that wasn't an option either. Not to mention the disturbing stranger who had broken into her home a week ago.

Kat had come home from yet another day of intense questioning at the station. She'd gone through her new normal routine to avoid the press, sneaking through the gardens and letting herself in at the back door. To her horror, a man had been sitting in her kitchen, a complete stranger drinking her tea, with no sign of a break-in.

His warning had been brief and chilling; she should keep her mouth shut or he would be back. And he would be very angry if that happened.

Kat had been just about coping with everything up until then, but his threat had tipped her over the edge. She'd packed her bag that night and moved into Paul's spare room without telling him why. So — going back to the house she'd shared with Nathan wasn't an option.

Now she slipped between some parked wagons and took out her phone, calling DI Paul Stafford, her boss and quite possibly the only friend she had left on the force. She got his voicemail.

'Paul? It's me. I hate to ask but can I kip at your place for a bit? Just tonight. And maybe tomorrow.'

Beyond that she had no idea. Thankfully her suspension came with full pay, so money wasn't a problem, for the moment at least. But keeping a low profile definitely was.

About to hang up, she hesitated, tempted to ask him to check the local hospitals to see if a blonde woman in her late twenties had been admitted.

But Paul would want to know why. And a question like that felt like a betrayal of her circus friends.

'Thanks, Paul,' she finished. 'Speak soon.'

Kat had taken a single step back towards the more public area when a man stepped between the two wagons, blocking her path. She recognised the guy who was staying in Delilah's caravan.

'What are you doing back here?' he demanded.

Kat slipped her phone into her pocket.

'That would be none of your business. Excuse me,' she said politely. 'Can I get past?'

He leaned an arm on one of the wagons.

'What's your hurry? Maybe you and I can have a little fun.'

Seriously? Kat wasn't in the mood for this.

'Move,' she told him.

The way behind her was clear. She could easily retreat. But that would have been running away and Kat had done enough of that recently. When he didn't step aside, she walked towards him, ready to shoulder past if she had to.

He made a grab for her and she reacted on instinct, catching his raised arm and using his own momentum to spin him round. A second later his arm was twisted up his back, his cheek pressed against the side of the wagon.

'I don't know who you think you are,' she said in his ear. 'But FYI, this kind of behaviour is not acceptable. Ever. Understood?'

He swore viciously and she tightened her grip on his arm until he cried out.

'Ow! Yes! Yes, OK.'

She let him go, stepping swiftly back to a safe distance in case of retaliation.

He glared at her, rubbing his arm, murder in his eyes. Then he glanced over her shoulder and froze.

* * *

Jake had been looking for Kat when he'd spotted Darrius's man, Finn, slip between the wagons, no doubt on his way to commit some petty larceny.

It had seemed like common sense to follow and when he'd seen the other man lunge at Kat, he'd stopped in shock. But he'd barely made a move to intervene when Kat had Finn in an arm lock.

If Jake hadn't seen it he would never have believed the speed with which it happened.

'All OK?' He looked from one to

the other.

'Everything's fine,' said Kat. Her face was flushed, but that was the only hint that anything untoward had just happened. She wasn't even breathing hard. 'Just a misunderstanding.'

Jake got why Finn might want to keep quiet about being bested by a woman, but why was Kat covering for him?

'Don't you have work to do?' he asked Finn.

Finn's reply was clenched fists and a glare that might have withered another man.

Jake squared his shoulders and subtly shifted his weight, his own fists closing as the tension thrumming through him for the past few days roiled up, suddenly eager for an outlet.

Whatever Finn saw in Jake's expression, he seemed to decide that being elsewhere was a good idea. Spitting on the grass, he stalked away.

Jake was almost sorry. Yet he couldn't risk any trouble. Any more trouble. At least Finn's humiliation might stop him reporting to Darrius.

'So?' he said to Kat. 'You'll be on your way?'

'I suppose.'

'Actually I was looking for you,' he told her. 'I have some stuff of your dad's you might like. It's back at the office if you want to take it with you?'

'You have?' Her eyes lit up, giving him a glimpse of the old Kat, not this lost-looking stranger. For a second he imagined wrapping her in his arms, telling her everything was going to be all right, that nothing was ever as bad as it seemed.

But if the past few days had taught him anything it was that things were definitely not all right and the future might well be even worse.

The light went out of her eyes as fast as it came.

'Maybe I should wait until I have somewhere to keep it,' she said glumly.

What had gone so wrong in her life? Jake wondered. She was already looking better after a night's sleep and a decent meal. How might she look after a week of being looked after by friends, away from what was troubling her? But he hardened his heart; whatever Kat's problems, they would not be improved by staying here.

'Why don't I show you? We're pulling down tonight. We might be less easy to find in the future.'

'OK,' she agreed.

Together they began walking towards the small caravan that served as an office for the circus.

'Where are you going next?' she asked.

As soon as Jake had mentioned pull down, he'd realised his mistake. But there was no point in lying. She could find out from anyone.

'Huntersly.'

Her fleeting smile returned.

'Lord Huntersly still lets you pitch on his land?'

'For now, yes. So where did you learn to do that?' he asked, neatly changing the subject.

She glanced at him sideways. 'Do what?'

'The arm lock.'

'Ah. You saw that.' Embarrassment

brought some much-needed colour back to her cheeks. 'A girl has to pick up skills in the real world.'

It disturbed him to think of her living in a world where that sort of skill was necessary.

'Who is that guy anyway?' she continued. 'He's a menace.'

Jake knew he should probably come up with a story but there had been enough lies.

'Darrius brought some of his men with him as part of the deal. I presume they work for him and he doesn't want them sitting idle while he's away. Turns out he doesn't employ them for their brains.'

'Does one of them run the ticket booth?'

'Yes, why?'

She told him about yesterday's rudeness.

'Thanks,' he said grimly. 'I'll deal with it.'

As they neared the small office caravan, Jake's heart sank, seeing Darrius sitting on the steps.

5

Jake only just resisted rolling his eyes heavenward. Seriously? Could this day get any worse?

'Ah, Jacob. You've arrived.' Darrius leaned on his silver-topped cane — an affectation, Jake knew; the man was fitter and faster than his build suggested. Today, as well as the cane, Darrius also sported a broad-brimmed fedora.

'We have an appointment, I understand.'

'We agreed to meet at eleven,' said Jake flatly. 'So, if you'll excuse us —'

Darrius ignored him and tipped his hat to Kat.

'Still here, I see? My man Finn says he saw you sneaking around, whispering into your phone.'

'Not sneaking. And not whispering,' said Kat easily. 'And you can tell your man Finn I'll break his arm if he touches me again.'

Darrius threw back his head and laughed.

'Feisty. I can see why you like her, Jacob. Though a little bird tells me you slept with the horses last night. Why is that, I wonder? Losing your touch?'

'As I said, our arrangement was for eleven o'clock,' grated Jake. 'I have something I have to do first, Darrius. Why don't we meet by the car?'

'I'll wait.' Darrius simply smiled.

Jake swallowed his frustration. But as the whole point of chasing Kat off was to keep her away from this man, he wasted no time arguing but unlocked the door of the tiny caravan. The inside was piled with boxes of invoices and receipts, a sight that filled him with dread. Kat stuck her head in, but then waited outside with Darrius.

Jake would very much have preferred to give her the mementoes of her father in private, but it seemed that wasn't to be. In which case, he should just do it as quickly as possible.

He found the box under the desk and

carried it outside, wordlessly holding it out.

She didn't take it but opened the lid and peered inside, going very still.

'What is it?' Darrius nosied in.

Jake saw tears gather in Kat's eyes, saw her throat bob as she swallowed, seemingly unable to look away from the contents of the box.

'Kevin left them,' said Jake quietly. 'He's been using them all this time but they belonged to your dad and he thought you should have them.'

Kat just nodded.

Darrius however wasn't similarly moved. He plucked the high-topped, black silk hat and bull whip, out of the box and immediately swapped his fedora for the topper.

'You should have given these to me, Jacob. I could have put them to good use. Was your father a ringmaster?' he asked Kat.

She tried to snatch the top hat off his head but Darrius evaded her.

'My father wasn't just ringmaster,' she

said hotly. 'He started this circus.'

And there it was; exactly what Jake had been trying to avoid.

Darrius frowned.

'Your father started . . .' His eyes widened. He glanced at Jake then back at Kat, so distracted he allowed her to snatch the hat off his head. 'Do you mean . . . are you telling me . . . your mother was Mara Turnado?'

'Yes. What has that got to do with anything?'

Jake could only watch as the world collapsed around him. So much for keeping her safe.

'So that . . .' Darrius was still working it out. But the smile that split his face when he did reminded Jake of a shark. 'That makes you Kat Turnado?'

Kat nodded, warily.

'What a stroke of luck,' said Darrius. 'This changes everything, eh, Jacob? Ms Turnado, if I'd only known yesterday . . . I would have been . . . I mean, this is wonderful. Just wonderful! And to think you were going to let her leave,

Jacob. Ms Turnado, I simply insist you stay.'

His meaty fingers dug deep into Jake's tense muscles, issuing a warning which Jake ignored.

'This is a business, Darrius,' he said. 'We can't afford any baggage —'

'I can work,' said Kat quickly and his stomach dropped further. She glanced into the office. 'Even if it's just to sort out those invoices.'

'Yes, paperwork is not Jacob's forte, I fear. But that's settled,' said Darrius heartily. 'Ms Turnado, Jacob and I were about to make a little trip. I would like very much for you to join us.'

Jake made one last desperate attempt. 'Since I'll miss the afternoon performance, Kat could make herself useful here —'

Darrius' silver eyes glittered a warning.

'You're not listening, Jacob. I insist she comes.'

* * *

Kat trotted after Jake and Darrius to where the circus people parked their private cars.

Jake's anger was obvious to all and Kat felt a tad guilty that she'd wangled her way into a job despite his best efforts. But she refused to feel sorry. Having nowhere to stay was not a pleasant position to be in, and besides, she was confident she really could make herself useful.

Darrius swaggered along swinging his cane, looking like the cat who had swallowed the canary.

Without last night's stage make-up and fake moustache, the ring master looked completely different. His face was round and smooth, almost cherubic in its softness. But while his striking grey eyes appeared smaller without their smear of kohl, they were no less keen and intelligent.

Yet there was something off about his beaming benevolence, and Kat knew she wasn't the only one to sense it. She'd seen it in Nellie's nervous twitching and Phaedra's scowl. And she could see it right now in Jake's tense, stiff-shouldered march.

The million dollar question was; why did the no-nonsense circus folk defer to Darrius so much? And why had Jake given him so much power? Just how much had he invested in Circus Mara?

'Where are we going?' she asked him.

'Huntersly Hall,' said Darrius. 'I believe you are familiar with the place?'

Of course she was. The Huntersly Estate was a prime site and a real coup for Circus Mara. No other circus was ever allowed to pitch there.

'So his Lordship is still there?' she asked, pleased. The Lord Huntersly she had known growing up was a big circus fan, but had been an even bigger fan of Kat's mother. Only as Kat had grown older had it become obvious to her that his family disapproved of the connection. And seriously disapproved of something as common as a circus being allowed on their land.

Yet Lord Huntersly had ignored all advice and become a good friend to her family. He'd been devastated by the accident.

Jake remained stonily silent. Darrius answered.

'Yes. Lucky for us, eh?'

They stopped beside a new-looking Range Rover with tinted rear windows. Darrius' personal car presumably, as he tossed the keys to Jake, who caught them one-handed.

'Why don't you drive, Jacob? Ms Turnado can sit upfront with you.'

'Why are we going to Huntersly now?' Kat asked Jake as she climbed into the passenger seat. 'I thought pull down was tonight?'

Surely he would have spoken to his lordship and sorted out all the details days ago.

Again Jake maintained a stony silence and she wondered if he was sulking.

'It seemed like the friendly thing to do,' said Darrius. 'Since his lordship is doing us such a favour. We just want to double-check some of the security arrangements. Besides, the visit will allow you and him to catch up, won't it?'

Kat didn't point out that now she was staying with the circus, she could catch up with Lord Huntersly any time over the next few days.

* * *

Huntersly Hall was about a three-hour drive away. Kat liked to think that if she and Jake were alone in the car, the tension between them might have let up a bit and they would have found some common ground or called a truce. But Darrius' overbearing presence made that impossible, and half of the journey passed in almost total silence.

Until her phone rang.

When her ex-fiancé was first arrested, Kat had watched helplessly as their home was searched by blank-faced colleagues who wouldn't meet her eye. Her phone and laptop were seized along with all of Nathan's electronics, and she had no idea when — or if — she would ever get hers back.

That meant only two people had her new number. Eagerly she pulled her phone out, disappointed when the name on screen wasn't Delilah's.

'Paul?' Darrius read the screen over her shoulder. 'Oh dear. You may have a rival, Jacob.'

Kat would have preferred to speak to her boss without an audience in case he had news about her suspension. But she knew he'd only worry if she didn't pick up.

'Hey, kid,' said Paul cheerfully. 'How are you holding up?'

'Fine.' She cupped her hand around her phone but had no idea how much Jake or Darrius could hear. 'I can't really talk right now.'

'Me neither,' said Paul and she heard traffic noises and a car door close. 'Just on my way to a job. But I wanted to let you know it's no problem for you to stay at mine. Beth and the kids are at her sister's, so stay as long as you like.'

'Thanks.' Kat was grateful for his offer but knew that with three kids and a sweet but long-suffering wife, it was an imposition. Plus, if the guy who'd broken into her house was still looking for her, she had no intention of bringing trouble to Paul's door.

'Things have changed again, though. I'm going to hang around here for a bit,' she said.

She could picture Paul's face as he suddenly paid closer attention. 'Everything OK, kid?'

'Everything's great. I mean it. I'll ring you.'

'Any time,' he said and disconnected.

Darrius was still leaning forward in his seat.

'Who was that?' he asked conversationally.

'Just a friend,' said Kat.

'Darrius!' Jake interrupted, nodding towards the rear view mirror. Darrius turned. Kat could have sworn everyone in the car was holding their breath as a police car, lights flashing, bore down on them.

6

The police car sped past them and the rest of the journey proceeded in silence until they reached the gates of Huntersly.

Again Darrius leaned forward, this time examining the sturdy metal gates and the high stone walls. Kat could see a very visible security camera trained on them but suspected there would be several more, less visible, cameras also watching.

Jake rolled down his window and spoke into an intercom. His face would be on camera, she realised suddenly, and hers too. Whereas Darrius in the back, with tinted windows and his ridiculous hat, would be much less visible.

'Jake Romero and Darrius Bell from Circus Mara,' said Jake. 'We have an appointment to see Lord Huntersly.'

'And the other passenger?' asked a voice.

'Kat Turnado, also from Circus Mara,' said Jake.

'One moment please.' They had to wait before the gates rolled back, on smooth and silent runners.

'Open sesame,' said Darrius softly

Jake drove down a long driveway. The house was shielded from the road by a tangle of exuberantly flowering rhododendrons. Then the view opened up to beautifully landscaped gardens, with the impressive Huntersly Hall in the middle.

Kat couldn't help but admire the gothic magnificence of the old house; the embellished colonnades at the entrance, the sculpted mouldings and high spires on each wing.

On one side of the house a meticulously manicured lawn gradually gave way to a wildflower meadow, which sloped gently down to a lake. The circus would pitch its tent in the meadow.

As a child Kat had been left speechless at the sheer size and magnificence of Huntersly Hall. Now, though, looking at the old building, another memory was triggered. Had she seen the house more recently? On TV? Perhaps a location for a period drama? She wasn't sure.

The Earl of Huntersly himself waited at the top of the steps to greet them. He had aged in the years since Kat had last seen him and was leaning on a cane, but his smile and the twinkling mischief in his blue eyes were the same as ever.

'Kat? Is that really you? Oh my goodness. Little Kat!' He threw his arms around her. 'I can't believe it. Let me look at you. Oh my. You look so much like your mother! Come in, come in. Can I offer you tea? Coffee? Lunch?'

'We're just here to check the ground,' said Jake at the same time as Darrius stepped forward and said, 'Coffee would be very welcome. How kind.'

Lord Huntersly looked at him. 'And you are, sir?'

Darrius gave a little bow. 'Darrius Bell, Circus Mara's newest ringmaster. It is an honour to meet you, your Lordship.'

Lord Huntersly beamed. 'The pleasure is all mine. What a wonderful job you do have, if I may say so. I cannot wait to see the show. Cannot wait, sir. Follow me, please. Kat if I'd known you were coming I'd have had Mrs Booth make those little cakes you used to like so much.'

He led them through the massive doors into a spacious, marble-tiled hall. It hadn't changed a bit since Kat was a child but then she supposed houses like this tended not to change in centuries.

'We'll take coffee in the library, thank you, Jamieson,' said Lord Huntersly to a man in a dark suit who was hovering nearby.

The butler nodded politely and moved to obey but Kat didn't miss his expression. It was one she'd once been used to but hadn't seen for years; the distrust many people held for the circus.

She suspected Jamieson had never approved of them being here — certainly not being treated as honoured guests. He, however, had at least always been polite. Unlike Lord Huntersly's two sons.

The old man seemed to pick up on her thoughts.

'Do you remember how you used to play here with the boys?' He chuckled. 'The floor was lava or crocodiles or some such and no one could touch it. They jumped from chair to sofa but you scampered up the bookcases like a little monkey.'

Kat did remember. She'd climbed the bookcases to get away from Marcus and Hector who were not only much older than her, but terrible snobs who had teased 'the circus brat' mercilessly. They'd been no match for a child raised in a circus, though. They'd never once caught her. Kat had perched on top of the bookcase and hurled books at them, laughing at their attempts to reach her.

'I do.' She smiled, filled with affection for the sweet old man.

Jake still hadn't said a word by the time the refreshments arrived; tea and coffee, along with a tray of sandwiches and cake. Lord Huntersly waved Jamieson away and poured the tea himself.

Kat didn't understand what was going on with Jake. He'd never been a sulker; on previous visits here when the pair of them had stood in for her parents, he'd seemed to get on well with Lord H.

'Do either of you two gentlemen know how I met Kat's mother?' asked Lord Huntersly once the butler had departed and they were settled, balancing no doubt priceless china cups and saucers in their laps.

Jake and Darrius shook their heads. Kat, who had heard the story before, allowed her attention to wander. Looking around the library she again had the impression she had seen the room recently.

'. . . riding in the woods when I saw a woman on a glorious white horse. Riding in our private woods, mind, bold as brass. Goodness knows how she got in. She was the most beautiful creature you have ever seen, so delicate and small-boned atop this massive brute who was prancing and sidestepping and snorting fit to burst.

'I was concerned. Not just because she was where she shouldn't be, but because her ride looked far too much horse for such a delicate woman to handle. I approached and offered my assistance as any gentleman would. The look she gave me!' He laughed at what was clearly a fond memory. 'Complete disdain. She didn't say one word to me but spoke to the horse. Suddenly it started dancing. Dancing! Next minute she jumped to her feet on the horse's back — on his back, I say! — and they galloped off without a backward glance. By the time I got over the shock, I had no chance of catching them.

'Of course, when I heard the circus was in town I knew this enchanting creature must have come from there. I had to see her again. And she was just as beautiful.' He sighed. 'I'd have married her in an instant, you know, given up all this for her. But alas, she was spoken for — to my mother's relief, I should add. In another time I'd have challenged your father to a duel for her hand.' Another chuckle. 'But we all became friends. And remained friends until . . .' His eyes clouded with grief and suddenly he looked his age. 'Well, you know.'

Suddenly it came to her.

'The painting!' said Kat. 'I saw you on the news when they discovered that old masterpiece.'

Lord Huntersly beamed.

'Yes indeed. We were quite famous for a while,' he said modestly. 'But do you recall which painting it was, my dear?'

Kat shook her head. Her life had been hectic at the time, both with work and keeping up with Nathan's busy social life.

'It was the portrait of The Lady,' beamed Lord Huntersly.

As a child Kat had loved the small oil on canvas of a young woman lying on her bed, eyes closed, her head resting on a silk pillow. It was so very different from the other dull, dark paintings of severe-looking men on horses or women with high, silly wigs. This one had always felt as if the subject was a real person who had lived and been loved. Kat had spent hours staring at it, wondering who The Lady, as she'd called her, was, whether she was dreaming and if so, of what.

'The Tintoretto,' burst out Darrius, making everyone jump. Everyone but Jake, Kat noticed. For a man with a tan he suddenly looked very pale.

'Sorry,' Darrius apologised. 'But I too remember seeing it on the news. What a wonderful discovery.'

'It was indeed,' agreed Lord Huntersly. 'No one knows where it came from, you see. It's just always been there, even when I was a boy. To be honest we've never paid it much attention. But Marcus, my son, had a friend staying — an art historian. He was very curious about the painting and, well, as you say, after a lengthy authentication process it has been accepted as a hitherto unknown Tintoretto. They think it's a portrait of his daughter. On her deathbed, unfortunately.'

'Oh.' Kat very much preferred her version.

'May we see it?' asked Darrius eagerly.

'We need to get back.' Jake sounded desperate. 'And we still have to inspect the field.'

Darrius turned steely grey eyes on him.

'I'm sure it will only take a moment or two, Jacob. And who could pass up such an opportunity?'

'By all means,' said Lord Huntersly. He indicated the far wall.

'You mean . . .' Darrius' jaw dropped and he leaped to his feet. 'That's it? The original?'

'Yes. But please don't get too close. There are all sorts of security doodahs in place. Pressure pads and lasers, can you believe. If you trip an alarm, all hell will break loose.' Lord Huntersly winked at Kat. 'As this silly old fool knows to his cost.'

Darrius stepped lightly across the room and stopped several feet from the painting, glancing back questioningly.

'Yes, that's probably close enough,' confirmed his lordship. 'Sorry. The insurance company . . .'

'Didn't like the circus coming,' Kat finished for him.

His face flushed. 'I vouched for you, of course . . .'

'Don't be silly,' said Kat. 'You can't know every single one of us.'

'Marcus wanted to put in in a safe,' muttered his lordship. 'But I refused. This is still my home and the painting is being sent to auction in a few weeks. She's hung here a long time. I refuse to have her moved until she has to be.' He sighed. 'I resisted selling, too, but Marcus has his heart set on some major renovations to make the old place more profitable . . .'

'I understand,' said Kat, smiling. Jake still didn't look great. Meanwhile Darrius, she noticed, wasn't actually looking at the painting at all. His gaze was darting to the celling, the walls, the windows.

Jake was looking at the carpet. Kat had a very bad feeling about this. She stood up.

'Well, thank you for the refreshments but we've taken up enough of your time.'

'Oh, I'm sure —' began Darrius but Kat was firm.

'We really should go. Thank you for everything,' she continued, taking both Lord Huntersly's hands.

'You do look so very like your mother, my dear,' he said, misty-eyed.

The butler showed them out, closing the door firmly. On the steps Darrius took out his phone.

'You two go and do whatever you have to. I have some calls to make. Don't take too long.'

Kat and Jake crossed to the meadow. She doubted he needed to do anything. They'd pitched here for years and the ground was sound.

Kat stopped abruptly and waited until Jake noticed and turned back.

'Are you ready to tell me what's going on?' she asked.

He looked at her for a long moment, his green eyes troubled and she held her breath, certain that he was finally going to say something.

Then the shutters came down once more.

'No.'

Walking back towards Darrius she was very aware of the fact he hadn't denied there was something going on. Only that he wasn't going to tell her what.

7

Jake seethed as he drove back. Could Darrius have been more obvious? The man clearly wasn't nearly as clever as he thought he was. Or maybe he just didn't care?

He'd certainly aroused Kat's suspicions. She was studying him far too closely. Jake could only hope to keep them apart as far as possible.

Just something else to add to a list of problems that was threatening to overwhelm him.

Back at the circus, the matinée performance was just coming to an end. Jake parked and leapt out, eager to go and check that everything was running smoothly. Darrius stopped him.

'A very pleasant morning, Jacob, don't you think?' he said affably.

Ignoring him, Jake kept walking resolutely.

'And you too, Ms Turnado. Thank

you for your company.' Darrius tipped his hat and strolled away.

'Jake?' Kat hurried after him. 'Um, do you have any idea where I'll be sleeping? Or what you would like me to do?'

'Leave?' he suggested.

'Ha ha.'

He stopped and pinched the bridge of his nose.

'Sorry. You'll be staying in my caravan. All the others are full.'

Sharing his caravan with her every night, being that close to her, would be torture but he consoled himself that it wasn't as if he was sleeping much anyway these days.

She didn't seem any more keen on the plan than he was.

'Even the bunk wagon?'

Every travelling circus kept a wagon fitted out for itinerant staff, labourers or foreign acts that were here to train or to teach.

Jake was exasperated.

'Do you really think I'm going to put you in the bunk wagon? With your connection to this circus? Don't worry, I called and asked Nellie to clear out my spare bedroom for you. It's fine. I'm sure we can stay out from under each other's feet.'

'OK, thanks,' she said. 'And what do you want me to do? Now that I work here.'

He was still marching towards the big top with Kat trotting along beside him.

'You'll have to hit the ground running. Why not start by taking over the ticket booth for this evening's performance? I'll find something else for that muppet Dmitri to do.'

He knew she had worked the ticket booth before.

'OK, that's fine. And later? Long term, I mean?'

'We'll talk,' he said and was gone.

Well, it wasn't a welcome-to-the-family but she was staying and she had a job. Kat would take her victories where she could get them.

She checked her watch. For most people the time between the day and evening show was downtime, used to catch up with domestic chores or to spend time with the family. Even so, there was usually plenty to occupy a willing pair of hands.

Maybe Phaedra would appreciate some help? Kat might be rusty, but at least she'd never let a horse go and have to chase it round a field.

But first she'd go to Jake's caravan and unpack her meagre belongings. That was a major regret about the life she'd left behind — that she'd left in such a rush, she hadn't packed enough clothes.

Well — no. Not her most major regret. But she hoped and prayed that her biggest regret would never come to light.

* * *

Kat easily found Jake's caravan, wondering again how he'd managed to afford such a high-end model. As she approached, the door opened and Nellie tossed a couple of black bin bags onto the grass, then reached behind her for a third.

'Let me give you a hand with that,' offered Kat.

Nellie jumped at the sound of her voice and to Kat's shock, she realised her friend was crying.

'Nellie! What's wrong?'

In reply Nellie dropped the bag she was holding and threw her arms around Kat, hugging her close.

'Oh lovey, I don't know what to do. I can't bear this.'

'Can't bear what?' asked Kat gently. 'Tell me what's happened?'

'Jake messaged,' sobbed Nellie. 'To ask me to clear everything out of his spare room. That can only mean one thing. I'm worried something terrible must have happened.'

Kat realised that no one knew yet that she was working here.

'Well, I hope it's not terrible, but you're clearing it out for me. I'm going to be staying for a bit. I am sorry if that means more work for you. I can take over if you like?'

Nellie cocked her head. 'You're

staying?' she asked. 'That's why I'm clearing this stuff out?'

'Yes,' said Kat. 'I'm sorry if that upsets you.'

'Of course it doesn't upset me!' Nellie's mood changed instantly. 'You staying is wonderful news. But I'm going to kill Jake!'

'Why?'

'For making me think —' Nellie caught herself. 'Never mind. Men!' she huffed.

Still muttering she bent to pick up her bags but as she did so one of them burst open spilling candy-pink clothing all over the grass. Kat picked up a spangly body stocking in a pink so shocking it could only belong to one person.

'Why are Delilah's clothes in Jake's caravan?' she asked, mystified. And then the obvious answer hit her. 'Oh.'

Jake and Delilah were an item? Was this the big news Delilah had wanted to share with her?

Actually that explained a lot — especially why everyone was so cagey about telling her anything.

'What happened?' she asked, not ready to explore how she felt about the news. 'Did they have a row? Is that why she's gone? Sorry,' she said quickly when Nellie didn't reply. 'I don't mean to put you on the spot. It's none of my business.' Flustered, she handed the body stocking to Nellie. 'We both know what Del's like. She'll be back when she calms down.'

Nellie looked desperate to say something.

'Yes. That's right. She'll be back,' she said fiercely. 'I know she will.' She gathered up the other bags. 'I'm glad you're here, lovey,' she told Kat. 'And I know Jake is too, despite all his nonsense. Poor lamb takes everything on himself, but then he always did, like when your dad —'

She snapped her mouth shut and scurried off.

Utterly baffled, Kat watched her go.

* * *

Kat had no qualms about ousting Dmitri from the ticket booth, and she did a brisk job selling tickets for the evening show. Once the flap closed on the Big Top and the show was underway, she slipped inside to watch.

There was always an air of excitement for the last show on a pitch. Everyone made an extra effort, or that's what it seemed like to Kat.

Tonight's show started with a Diabolo act. The Diabolo was a piece of wood shaped a bit like an egg timer with a metal axle in the middle, which was spun and tossed on a string tied to two hand-held sticks. Once in motion it could be thrown and caught, or made to travel up and down the string in apparent defiance of gravity. The teenager in the ring performed the intricate manoeuvres like a pro.

Next came the clowns. Nellie had told her over dinner that she didn't perform in the ring as often now she was 'getting on a bit.' Noodle was still as active as ever and was training up their young nephew, who was desperate to join the circus. But the boy was sitting exams this week — a condition set by his non-circus mother, who was hoping to send her son down a different path.

So this evening Noodle did a solo routine. A classic, Kat recognised, as he walked into the centre of the ring carrying a violin.

The lights went down and a spotlight came on as he started to play a haunting melody. Just as the audience began to get restless, the spotlight moved a few feet to the left. Without missing a note, Noodle followed it. But it moved again. And again.

Each time, it moved faster, or to somewhere ridiculous like into the audience or halfway up a ladder. Noodle followed doggedly. At one point he wobbled across a high wire as he chased the wandering spotlight, still playing manfully.

The kids loved it. Kat found herself laughing too.

She watched an escapology act by two young Italian men whom she'd never met. Her heart was in her mouth as she waited for one of them to burst free after being chained in a tankful of water.

To her relief, Jake didn't repeat the Wheel of Death. Marty's usual partner had been in hospital yesterday while his wife gave birth. Tonight the proud dad was back in his rightful place, leaping and jumping and defying death while his wife and baby son waited in their caravan.

The new father could not wipe the smile off his face, his happiness infecting everyone around him.

One by one, the acts continued. Some were familiar, tried and true, some brand new to Kat.

Jake performed a trapeze act with two highly talented young women. As they threw themselves gracefully into the air, he was always in the right place ready to catch them, steady and strong and utterly essential to their more spectacular efforts.

There were a couple of acts she was sure she could help with. Noodle, especially, might take her on while his nephew was studying. And she was sure she could revive an act she'd once done with Captain if the old macaw was amenable.

But tonight was not the time to raise these thoughts with anyone. Even before the last audience member was out of the tent at the end of the show, men had moved in and started folding and dismantling the tiered seats. The ring, too, was swiftly removed and packed in sections onto a waiting wagon.

Kat had already noticed various pieces of equipment being stowed away as it was finished with in the evening's show. Within a shorter time than seemed possible, the tent itself began to come down. Things had moved on since her dad's day and no brute force was needed as a new hydraulic system did all the hard work.

Even with the heavy lifting taken care of, the big top was massive, and heavy, and all hands were needed on deck before it too was safely stored away in a wagon.

Normally after pull down everyone hitched up their caravans, piled into the lorries and trucks and began an orderly evacuation of the field, driving through the night to reach tomorrow's pitch so the tent could be raised before breakfast.

Not tonight, though. First of all Huntersly Hall was only a three-hour drive away. But secondly, because of the security set up at the Hall, it had been agreed they'd arrive early next morning rather than after dark. The security company did not want to be checking IDs in the middle of the night.

Kat mucked in, doing whatever she could until the last concession stand was packed, the last burger van scrubbed. But she was still back at Jake's caravan long before he was.

She was in bed, though not quite asleep, when he arrived. His footsteps paused outside her door but then moved on.

Drifting off, she replayed the day in her head. Darrius checking out the security at the hall. There was something very off about the man.

And Jake and Delilah. What did she think of that? She was happy for them. Wasn't she?

Still telling herself that, she drifted off to sleep.

8

With pull down complete, everyone rose early the next day and breakfast was mostly eaten on the move.

Jake was up and out before Kat stirred but she found him wolfing down bacon sandwiches at Nellie's. His check shirt was dusty, the sleeves rolled up. Kat had the impression he had already been working for hours.

'Is there anything in particular you want me to do today?' she asked, pouring herself some coffee.

'Can you tow my caravan?' he asked promptly. 'Assuming you've kept your licence up to date?'

She nodded.

'Good. I'd like to go on ahead and be at Huntersly when everyone arrives, in case of any trouble. Marty will show you which lorry to use and you'll find the keys on the board in the office.'

She headed to the little office caravan

to fetch the key. All the keys for the circus vehicles were kept here, along with spare keys for the private cars. There was plenty of coming and going in the caravan and Kat exchanged words with a few people who seemed genuinely pleased to hear that she was staying. She took a moment to survey the not-so-organised chaos of the caravan's filing system. Jake's living quarters were extremely neat and tidy. This workspace was not.

Dyslexia wasn't unheard of when they were children but none of the schools they had attended had considered it worth assessing the circus kids who expanded their classrooms every year. Jake had loathed school with a deep, abiding passion and skipped off any chance he could get. Even when he did attend, he talked back to the teachers or played the clown and was so disruptive he wasn't welcome anyway. It was only much later that Kat had come to understand how his undiagnosed problem had contributed to his wild reputation.

But she had seen the other side of him, too, his frustration when faced with a page of homework that she and Delilah could complete in minutes. His stubborn refusal to accept their help, and his embarrassment when the messy page of work he finally turned in was tossed back at him in disdain.

On those days he'd simply walk out of the classroom and when she got home from school Kat would find him with the horses or practising alone on the high wire. Give him something practical to do, and his patience and concentration were limitless. Paperwork, not so much.

A quick check through some of the files told her that someone — Delilah? — had kept things in some kind of order. But the end of the month was approaching and payday would need attending to. That was one thing she could definitely help with, at least until Delilah got back. She made a mental note to talk to Jake about it.

What she did not find in her admittedly cursory search was any sign of an injection of cash into the books from Darrius Bell.

* * *

She drove over to Jake's caravan, where Xerxes helped her hitch it up to the lorry. Already the field was emptying, with half the circus gone, leaving only pale, flattened grass.

Getting behind the wheel of such a large vehicle after so long was exhilarating. Or maybe it just felt good to be doing something useful again. Either way, Kat found herself grinning and singing all the way to Huntersly.

The drive was uneventful but when she arrived, she joined a long tailback of circus traffic waiting to get through the gates.

Security had always been tight here, even before the discovery of the Tintoretto. Huntersly Hall was not open to the public, and the house and contents were so valuable that special arrangements always had to be made to allow the circus access. Kat knew only the patronage of Lord Huntersly himself that allowed this to continue. After seeing how frail and old the Earl had become, she wondered how long they would be permitted to keep on coming.

For a while she sat patiently in her cab. But eventually, growing bored, she jumped down to join the others who were hanging about and muttering.

'When are we going to get the tent up at this rate?' grumbled one.

'Well, obviously we're a bunch of crooks and can't be trusted,' said another.

Kat could see why they were annoyed but she could see the other side, too. The checks were an insult but the truth was, while she loved her friends, not everyone in the circus was a fine upstanding citizen. Some were here because they had something to hide. A bit like her.

She made her way to the gates. Most of the circus people were out of their vehicles by now, their grumbling increasing by the minute on this warm spring day. Darrius and his men, she noticed, were still seated in his Range Rover. Keeping to themselves, or keeping a low profile?

Walking down the queue of vehicles, she made a quick call to Delilah. Still no answer. Should she leave a message? Tell her friend she knew about her and Jake and that she was OK with it? No, it was none of her business. Besides, she wasn't sure she was OK, which was ridiculous considering how long she'd been away. And that she'd been engaged to another man for part of that time.

At the gate, Jake and Lord Huntersly's eldest son were in the middle of a heated altercation.

'My people have passports, driving licences and DBS certificates,' snarled Jake. 'What more do you want? Besides, I can personally vouch for each and every one of them.'

'Well that makes all the difference,' sneered Marcus. 'The word of a man who wears Lycra to work has to carry some weight, I suppose.'

'At least he does work,' said Kat. 'Hello, Marcus. Still trying to make yourself feel important, I see.'

Jake scowled. 'Kat, I'm handling this.'

Recognition spread over Marcus' face. 'Well, well, if it isn't my father's feral kitten.' His sneer turned into a leer. 'And all grown-up, I see. Now you, I wouldn't mind seeing in Lycra.'

Kat saw Jake take an angry step forward.

'What a pity your father's charm skipped a generation,' she told Marcus sweetly, before turning to Jake. 'What's the hold-up?'

'The hold-up,' said Jake, 'is this jumped-up —'

Marcus spoke over him in lofty tones. 'Unfortunately we have to do a thorough security vetting. On everyone. I'm sure you understand that I have to be careful who I allow onto my land.'

'Your father's land,' Kat corrected him.

'Do you see my father here?'

'No. And I'm glad — he'd be ashamed of you.'

Marcus's lip curled.

'Just like you should be ashamed of your father?'

Kat frowned. 'What does that mean?'

'Enough!' said Jake swiftly. 'Can I remind you we are here by invitation,' he told Marcus.

'Yes, well, make the most of that. It could well be the last invitation you get.'

'Maybe so, but it's been issued and accepted,' said Jake. 'So are you going to let us in?'

'When the checks are done,' smirked Marcus.

'Fine.' Jake turned away. 'Phaedra,' he called. 'Unload the horses, will you? It's too hot for them in the horsebox and they need watered. Oh, and let the pygmy goats out, too. No need to build a pen, just try and keep them from jumping walls or wriggling through the barred gate. They could damage those flowers if they get into the grounds.

'Nellie, it looks as if we're going to be here for a while so can you set up a burger van and a tea truck over by the gate? Marty, what time did you say the press was coming? Maybe we can get a picture of his lordling here with the goats?'

'Fine!' snapped Marcus, his pasty skin flushed an angry red. 'I suppose it might be possible to speed things up a bit.' He stormed off to speak to the security men who had been standing around.

'Thanks for all your help,' Jake called after him.

'You are so bad,' Kat said as they watched Marcus leave. 'Considering the horsebox is climate controlled and has fresh running water. The goats were a nice touch, though. Do we even have any?'

'What do you think?' grinned Jake.

She laughed all the way back to her lorry.

* * *

Although Kat had broken no laws and was only under internal investigation at work, she still had butterflies in her stomach when the security man at the gate took her ID away to check it on a laptop.

He would find nothing, she knew, but still she was tense. Especially as he took his time.

Eventually he returned and she reached out of the cab window to take her ID back from him, but his fingers held onto it for just a second too long.

'Fancy a drink later?' he asked.

She resisted rolling her eyes.

'Busy, but thanks,' she said.

Jake was inside the gate now, close enough that he could intervene should any of his people be hassled. He spoke to each driver who passed and was in constant communication with Xerxes via walkie-talkie. Kat observed a smooth, well-run operation. Her father would be proud.

'Where do I go?' she asked, pulling up beside Jake.

'Follow the others. Xerxes will show you where to park, then if you could help Phaedra with the horses that would be great,' he said immediately. 'After that you could go with Nellie and check the posters are up in town. Darrius' guys were supposed to do it, but . . .' He shrugged eloquently.

Why, Kat wondered, with such a low opinion of Darrius and his men, did he give them space on the circus? But now was not the time to ask.

As she drove off, her route was lined with stacks of metal fencing, of the sort used for festivals and crowd control. Once erected they would encircle the whole circus.

That was normal from a safety point of view but Kat could see an extra ring of fencing, making it a double layer. Plus even more panels to funnel the audience from the gate to the box office.

No doubt this was Marcus' doing. He couldn't keep the circus and the Hall further apart if he'd built a prison wall. She made a mental note to see what she could do about it.

Xerxes was waiting for her. He pointed to a spot then guided her in. Kat leaped out to help unhitch the caravan, then drove the truck to where the others were parked, well out of the way.

Phaedra was easy to find. The horsebox doubled as a stable for all six horses, but one of the first jobs on a new site was always to build a paddock. Lord Huntersly, bless him, had provided a sturdy temporary structure. Phaedra and Marty were already unloading.

'Jake sent me to help,' Kat said.

'Great,' said Marty. 'Are you OK to take over while I go give a hand with the tent? With Jake at the gate we're short-handed.'

Erecting the big top was always the main priority on a new site. Quite simply, no tent, no show.

Due to the extra security checks there would be only an evening show today. But it was expected to be a sell-out. Huntersly, with its gorgeous backdrop, always attracted a different kind of audience.

'Go for it,' she said and he gratefully handed over the horse he was leading.

It wasn't until much later that she recalled Marcus' comment about her father.

9

It was a long and busy day, but raising the circus was a well-practised routine and everyone knew their job. By late afternoon things were more or less ready, with Jake and Xerxes making their final checks.

Kat had finished with the horses and was helping set up the concession stalls when Nellie came to find her.

'We're off into town to check the posters. Jake says you're coming along?'

'You bet. I need to some shopping, if that's OK?'

'Then we'll do a supply run,' agreed Nellie.

Noodle was waiting in the car, in full costume as ever. Kat half considered disguising herself but decided that would be overkill. At work, only Paul knew of her connection to the circus and it would be a huge leap for anyone else to link DS Lyn Turner with Katelyn — or Kat —

Turnado, circus performer extraordinaire. Besides, who would even give her a second glance with Noodle drawing all the attention?

She was delighted to see Captain in the back.

'You're coming too?' she asked as the old macaw sidled up and snuggled against her leg.

'He sulks if he's left alone,' explained Noodle. 'And there are few things more destructive than a sulky parrot. Last time we left him he got into the kitchen cupboards, ripped open a bag of oatmeal and gave himself a 'sand' bath. Can you imagine the mess? We couldn't even hose him down as he would have turned to porridge — he was scattering oats for days, every time he spread his wings.'

'Watch me,' said Captain amiably and Kat laughed.

'He's a real trouper, isn't he?' she said, stroking his bright feathers.

'He's certainly not enjoying retirement much,' agreed Noodle.

'Actually I wanted to talk to you

about that.'

Kat outlined her plans to revive an old act she had done with Delilah and Captain.

'Go ahead.' Noodle gave his permission. 'If he doesn't want to do it, he won't.'

As expected Dmitri and Finn had done a poor job with the posters. But with Kat, Noodle, Nellie and Captain all working as a team, that was soon remedied. Any shopkeeper who showed reluctance to display one in their window was quickly charmed by a few magic tricks or by Captain's raucous rendition of *Polly Put the Kettle On*.

Of course, it didn't hurt that the circus had a long and affectionate connection with the Hall and the townspeople.

'Those two men you sent were unbelievable,' huffed a newsagent. 'Barged right in and started ripping down the church coffee morning poster to put yours up. Then they mouthed off at me. I chucked them out and put the poster in the bin.'

'I am so sorry,' said Nellie, going into full damage control mode. Before long the newsagent was agreeing you couldn't get the staff these days.

Captain had started off on his usual perch on Noodle's shoulder but had quickly fluttered to the top of a newspaper rack to survey the premises.

'Cat,' he muttered and she glanced over to check that he wasn't baiting the large tabby that was asleep in the sunny window.

But Captain wasn't paying the tabby any attention. His scarlet head bobbed up and down as he pecked at the newspaper on the top rack.

Kat's blood chilled as she read the headline. *Organised Crime Boss Helping Police With Enquiries*.

There was a picture of Nathan at a wedding a few weeks ago, so blond, handsome and carefree. Kat remembered that day. Nathan was looking away from the camera, seeking her out in the crowd, eager to introduce her to his friends . . .

And there she was in the background,

actually the only person really in focus. She was smiling, her hand playing with the beautiful necklace Nathan had given her only that morning . . .

'Kat, Kat, Kat,' muttered Captain. 'Watch me.'

Fear lodged deep inside her as she understood the significance of the photo. It was taken at a private function, so someone had issued it to the press. Someone who wanted to send her a message. Or a warning.

Noodle and Nellie were reminiscing about the good old days with the shopkeeper but Noodle half-turned as Captain kept chanting.

'I'll get him.' Quickly Kat strode across the shop and offered her hand to Captain to hop on. He cocked his head, fixing one beady, intelligent eye on her, but made no move to co-operate.

She grabbed a bag of brazil nuts — his favourite — off a rack and tore them open.

Captain graciously stepped onto her outstretched hand. She gave him a nut then carried him to the counter while she paid for them.

Noodle shook his head when he saw her purchase. 'Was he begging again?'

'Not quite,' she said. More like blackmail. She breathed a sigh of relief when they left the shop.

Next stop was the supermarket. Noodle and Captain stayed in the car, squabbling over the brazil nuts while Kat and Nellie grabbed a couple of trolleys. Kat bought a few personal items, underwear and several T-shirts. Then she and Nellie filled two trolleys with supplies on Nellie's list.

As they drove out of town again, almost every shop sported a circus poster.

'Why does Jake allow those two numpties, Finn and Dmitri, to keep working?' asked Kat.

Nellie and Noodle exchanged a look.

'It's complicated,' he said and she had to settle for that.

* * *

Everyone had been working flat out since dawn but there was still a lot of day ahead of them — everything from training and developing new acts to designing and mending costumes and building props. Not to mention the evening's performance to be got through.

People were busy, but the big top itself was empty when Kat slipped inside. This time the space had an air of peace and calm, and the scent of fresh sawdust and crushed grass smelled like home.

The trapeze rigging was already in place, as was the high wire. A safety net had also been put up as Noodle's nephew was coming for a lesson later.

Kat checked the tent flap was closed behind her and wiped her sweating palms on her jeans as she approached the fixed metal ladder which led all the way to the roof of the tent.

Before beginning to climb, she kicked off her shoes and found a pair of soft leather slippers in a storage box. Then, taking a deep breath, she began to climb the ladder.

It was hard going, using muscles rarely needed in police work. But Kat knew she had to justify her place in the show and in order to do that, she had to know what she was capable of.

Her mouth was dry as she reached the first high wire, which was actually no more than ten feet off the ground. This one was mainly used by the clowns — Noodle had been known to ride a bike across it, carrying a tiny umbrella. Kat stalled, then forced herself to step out. Luckily, it took less time to find her balance than to find the courage to try.

Her father's voice sounded in her ears.

'*One foot in front of the other. Keep your mass directly over the rope. If you move even a little off-centre the rope will start to swing like a pendulum. That's it, sweetheart, you're doing great!*'

It was both a relief and a triumph when she reached the other side. But she was only ten feet above the ground and considering the way her heart was pounding, she seriously doubted she could handle anything higher.

But she had to know. Taking yet another steadying breath, she climbed to the next level. This was twenty-five feet above the ring. Her mouth was dry, even though sweat dampened her palms and trickled between her shoulder blades. She was careful not to look down.

The trapeze bar was hooked over the side of the platform. Kat took hold of the bar in one hand, with the other gripping the side of the platform just as she'd been taught. All she had to do was let go, reach and grab the bar with both hands and launch herself out.

Again she heard her father's voice.

'*The first swing is to overcome your fear. The second is for fun.*'

Kat licked her lips. Up here, the air felt different, still and hot. Closing her eyes, she remembered what it was like to stand here during a show. There were distractions, lights, people coughing and children fussing in the audience below, and ring hands moving equipment. You had to be able to withdraw inside yourself and let the distractions go.

And Kat couldn't do it. Even though her parents had fallen from the Wheel of Death, rather than the trapeze, all she could think about was that this was the view they had both seen before they had tumbled to their deaths.

Right here, right now, she had never felt so close to them and never missed them more.

She was frozen with fear. This was too dangerous. Why would anyone do this?

Eventually she managed to force herself to hook the trapeze bar back in place. She was about to attempt to climb down when she heard voices below. Looking down, she saw Jake with Darrius.

'One call a day,' said Jake. 'That was what we agreed.'

He sounded furious. Kat stood very still; if they didn't look up, they might not see her.

'Yes we did agree that, Jacob — but I'm having some technical problems. I assure you they will be rectified later today.'

Jake stepped closer to Darrius, until

he was right in his face. Kat could feel his simmering anger but Darrius, to his credit, stood his ground.

'They had better be. If you want us to stick to our side of the deal we expect you to do the same.'

'You say that as if you are actually in a position to bargain,' drawled Darrius.

'You have one hour,' said Jake.

'Until?'

'Until we decide we have nothing to lose.'

Darrius sauntered out, swinging his cane.

Kat was still puzzling over the exchange when Jake spoke.

'You can come down now,' he said.

She peered over the platform edge.

'How did you know I was up here?'

Jake nudged her shoes with his toe.

'Ah.'

His brow creased in concern.

'Can you get down?'

Just how bad did she look? The thought of him climbing up and carrying her down over his shoulder, was the shake she needed to get moving.

'Of course I can.'

It wasn't elegant but she made it.

Jake's concern deepened as he searched her face, and she could only imagine how pale and gross she looked.

'Are you OK?' he asked.

Kat could lie but there was no point. Not to Jake. She shook her head.

He touched her cheek, gently wiping a tear she didn't even know had fallen.

'There's no shame in being frightened, Kat.'

Yes, there was. Fear changed you. It tied your insides in knots, made you doubt your own beliefs.

The tenderness in his touch almost released a fresh burst of tears and she wrenched away.

'Are we going to ignore what I overheard?' she said, changing the subject.

Jake dropped his hand. 'Yes.'

'But —'

'We are not having this conversation, Kat.'

'Why not? I believe Darrius has some

kind of hold on you,' she persisted. 'On everyone here.'

There. She'd said it.

Jake looked at her steadily.

'So, I presume you were up there trying to figure out what acts you can help in? Do you want to perform in the ring, or work the concessions? If in the ring, what have you decided?'

He was just going to ignore her? OK, she knew what she'd said sounded ridiculous. But she also knew it was true.

'Well?'

Fine. She'd find out the truth on her own.

'I'd like to be back in the ring,' she told him. 'I think I'll be OK wire-walking as long as it's not too high. I'll need a few days to build up my agility and strength, so in the meantime I can continue to man the ticket booth. I've spoken to Noodle and he thinks we can devise an act together. But I can do juggling and diabolo, and I'm happy to step in anywhere I'm needed.'

Jake's eyes narrowed and she

wondered if she had given in too easily. Thankfully he nodded.

'Ask around. Ron Zappato was working on a perch act with Delilah. Maybe you can stand in?'

A perch act was all about strength and balance. She'd never tried it before but she'd seen it done.

'I'll talk to him.'

'And Xerxes' wife is pregnant and still at the throwing up stage. How's your nerve?'

Xerxes had a knife-throwing act. People took a lot of persuading to help with that one.

'With both feet on the ground, I'm sure my nerve is as steady as ever.'

'Good,' said Jake. 'And while I think about it, Delilah did an agility act with the pygmy goats. The little blighters are bored and keep getting out and causing havoc. They need to run off some of their energy. Can you do something with them?'

'I'll see what I can come up with. What about the payroll?' she suggested.

'I could make a start on that.'

Jake's sudden smile looked heartfelt.

'Anything you can do in the office is a godsend. Thanks,' he said and she knew he'd been worrying about it. Not that the great Jake Romero would ever admit to worrying about anything.

'I think that's enough to keep you busy. Plus, when word gets around that you're available I'm sure you'll be very much in demand.' He checked his watch. 'Sorry, got to go.' He hesitated. 'Actually, the local rag is coming. You don't want to be interviewed, do you? The prodigal returns and all that? It could make a good headline.'

'No, thank you.'

He had no idea the firestorm that could bring down on them.

10

Having decided to undertake her own investigation into what was going on, Kat was desperate to make a start.

That evening was their first show at Huntersly and she did a brisk trade in the ticket booth. She had hoped to sneak away once the show started and check out Darrius' caravan, but it wasn't to be.

'Kat, my dear.' Lord Huntersly was delighted to see her behind the counter. He was such a gent, he had joined the ticket queue until some locals recognised him and cheerfully pushed him to the front of the line. 'I would be honoured if you would join me to watch the show tonight, my dear.'

His Lordship was accompanied only by Jamieson the butler, not by either of his sons. How could she leave the pair of them to sit on their own?

'I'd love to,' she said and did just that.

During the interval she excused herself to sell hotdogs and when the show was over, she waited with his Lordship while Jamieson brought the car as close as he could — they were only a couple of hundred yards from the Hall, but the fence ringing the circus made it a much further walk, and it was obvious the old man wasn't up to it.

'This looks very pretty.' Lord Huntersly indicated the lights adorning the fences.

'Doesn't it?'

When Kat and Nellie had returned from their shopping trip, they had draped the ugly fencing with as many twinkling lights as they could rustle up. Which was a lot. Now that it was dark, the circus ground had been transformed into a wonderland.

After waving the old man off, Kat joined the clean-up. Darrius was apparently above this sort of menial task because he rarely lingered after a show. As he would no doubt be tucked up in his caravan by now or plotting his evil deeds, she had to abandon her plans for tonight.

If only she knew what those evil deeds were!

Once more she was late back to Jake's caravan and once more he was even later.

Kat had just stepped out of the small bathroom, wrapped in a towel with another, turban style over her hair, when the caravan door opened and he walked in.

She froze, clouds of steam billowing around her.

'Sorry,' said Jake, looking flustered. 'I should knock. I'm just not used to . . . I mean . . .'

'No. It's your home,' she said quickly. 'I'm the one who's sorry. I'll get out of your way.'

Jake's bedroom was behind her. To reach it, he had to squeeze past her. Clutching her towel tightly, Kat tried to sidestep in the narrow passageway. Unfortunately he did the same. There then followed one of those awkward 'dancing' moments which might have gone on for ever if they both hadn't realised and stopped.

He cleared his throat.

'I've just been locking up.'

'I've just had a shower.'

Really? Could she have said anything more obvious?

'Did Lord Huntersly enjoy the show?' asked Jake. 'I saw you sitting with him.'

'Yes.' She and Jake were almost touching. Kat's attention was unreasonably focused on his mouth, which was just inches away. 'He . . . he was like a little kid. It was lovely to see.'

Their eyes locked. His pupils darkened instantly.

'Are . . . are you responsible for the fairy lights everywhere?' He too seemed to be finding it difficult to concentrate.

'Yes.'

'That was a great idea. Thanks.'

'You're welcome.'

Still neither of them moved.

'Kat, I . . .'

'Yes?' she said eagerly.

The sound of a horse whinnying in

the distance broke the spell and awareness snapped back.

'Yes, well, I suppose . . .' He indicated his bedroom door.

The bedroom he shared with Delilah. At that reminder all impure thoughts fled from Kat's head.

She clutched her towel more tightly.

'Yes, me too. Time for bed. I mean my bed.'

She dived past him and into her room. Once inside, she stood with her back to the door, her breathing ragged.

How could she? How could she even have thought about kissing her best friend's boyfriend?

* * *

Mornings were always a busy time on a circus, which meant lots of people all rushing about. There was no chance of Kat getting near Darrius' caravan unnoticed so she decided to begin her investigation in the office, going through the books.

Her parents had started the circus in partnership with Kevin, the old ringmaster. After their death, overall responsibility had passed to Kevin but Kat knew from Delilah that Jake had taken over the day-to-day running of things even before Kevin's retirement last year. She was pleased to find the circus's finances looking surprisingly healthy under his watch.

What she did not find was any recent injection of cash. If Darrius wasn't an investor, who was he?

Her gaze fell on a battered wooden key cabinet on the wall. The circus kept duplicate keys for all the vehicles, including the caravans, in case anyone locked themselves out during a costume change. The cabinet was kept locked but she easily found the key where it had always been kept, under a snow globe souvenir of Scarborough.

She hadn't really expected Darrius' key to be here so she wasn't disappointed —

'What are you doing?'

'Ahhh!' She yelped at the sound of

Jake's voice. As casually as she could she locked the cabinet and returned the key to its rightful place. 'Someone should tie a bell on you!' she complained. 'Stop sneaking up on folk.'

'It's my office. No sneaking involved.'

He had a point.

'Sorry. Yes. You said I could tidy up in here, sort things out.'

'I did say that.' He glanced pointedly at the key cabinet.

'I'm just getting my bearings,' she said indignantly. 'Things could have changed in ten years. Anyway, I'm glad you're here. Do you have the password for the payroll?'

He looked at her for a long moment then took out his phone, unlocked it and opened a screen before handing it to her.

'What?' he asked dryly, seeing her expression. 'Surprised I don't have them on a scrap of paper?'

Actually she was. He had never been this organised before.

'Can I jot these down?'

'As long as you don't leave them lying around. Delilah forced me to embrace technology. She was a real help setting up systems I could work with.'

A flicker of dark emotion crossed his face.

'Do you miss her?' asked Kat.

'Of course I miss her! What a thing to say.'

'Then why aren't you doing more to find her?'

He blew out an exasperated breath.

'How do you know I'm not?'

'So you admit we should be looking for her, which means something is wrong! I can help.'

'How?' he asked bluntly. 'What can you possibly do that I can't?'

Now was the time to tell him that she was a trained investigator, but that would only lead to questions about why she was here and not at work.

'Keep out of it, Kat,' said Jake when she didn't answer. 'You have no idea what is going on.'

'Then tell me!'

But all he did was take his phone back and walk away.

* * *

The morning hadn't progressed her plans much but Kat was undeterred. She worked in the ticket booth for the matinee but as soon as the show was underway, she locked up, collected some supplies and headed for the corner of the horse paddock where the pygmy goats were penned.

Jake had given her the idea when he mentioned them yesterday. Now Kat opened a canvas bag she'd slung over her shoulder and crouched down to the level of the little creatures, scattering handfuls of Cheerios — their favourite snack. They raced over, bleating and butting each other.

Now they were all best friends, Kat opened the gate. With her bag of treats it was a given that they would follow her — though in anything but a straight line. However she managed to keep them moving in the general direction of Darrius' caravan.

Most of the circus folk were in or near the big top. Anyone Kat did encounter paid scant attention to someone walking a small herd of excited miniature goats around a circus ground.

His caravan was set apart from the others. And it wasn't facing inwards like the others — the door was angled towards Huntersly Hall.

Antisocial maybe, but it actually served Kat's purpose as she would not be in the direct line of sight of anyone approaching from the circus.

She didn't make a beeline for the caravan but meandered a bit. And under the pretence of keeping her bleating, leaping, skipping, leapfrogging pack in order, she was able to stop and check she wasn't being observed. Just a woman walking her goats.

As a final precaution she tossed a couple of handfuls of Cheerios on the ground around and under the caravan. The little goats went crazy, dropping to their knees and stretching their necks to reach them while Kat gently tried the door of the caravan.

Locked, of course, but it would have been foolish not to try. She was tempted to attempt to pick the lock there and then — growing up on a circus, she had acquired a collection of skills her parents had preferred not to know about — but she decided it was too risky. She'd never been nearly as good at picking locks as Noodle, her teacher, and if anyone saw her she had no excuse.

The goats were still madly foraging so she risked standing on tiptoe to peer in the caravan window, struck by the thought that Delilah might have been tied up and gagged inside all this time.

Nothing. Whew.

'Who let you lot out?'

She heard an angry voice behind her. Finn!

Kat reacted instinctively and dropped face down onto the grass, just as he rounded the caravan.

'Get away,' Finn told the gambolling

goats. 'These shoes cost a mint—' He broke off as he spotted Kat. 'You again. What are you doing here?'

'Oh, thank goodness you're here,' she said brightly, levering herself up to her knees and grabbing the nearest goat. 'I thought Branston here was stuck under the caravan but thankfully he's OK. Aren't you, sweetie?' She kissed the surprised goat on the forehead, beaming up at Finn. 'You're wondering why I call him Branston, aren't you? Well, it's because he's always in a pickle.'

'What're you talking about?' demanded Finn. 'Get up.' Suspicious, he tried the caravan door which didn't budge. 'I repeat. What are you doing here?'

'I'd say that's obvious.' She rose gracefully to her feet and dusted herself off. 'Rescuing goats. Any chance you could help me round them up?'

'Do I look like a bleeding goat herder to you? Get them out of here before I tell the boss.'

'Jake was the one who asked me to exercise them,' she said guilelessly.

'I'm not talking about Romero.' Finn's lip curled. 'Now clear off before I have to teach you a lesson for snooping.'

She couldn't resist. 'Would that be the same lesson you taught me last time?'

Finn didn't like that and Kat knew the time had come to bow out gracefully.

'OK, we're going. I hope they didn't make a mess. You might want to wipe your feet before going inside. Come on, boys and girls,' she called. With her hand in the bag of Cheerios, she didn't have to look to know the goats were following.

Sweat was trickling down her back and she had to force herself not to run. But she was smiling as she walked away.

She planned to sneak back later for a proper look, and the best time to do that was when Darrius was occupied in the ring.

11

After swapping places with Xerxes' wife Hazel, who was still in the throes of early pregnancy, Kat had been given a small part in that evening's show.

During more complex scene changes in a show, a team of female dancers would burst into the ring wearing eye-catching costumes, with the sole aim of distracting the audience from the boring but essential work going on around them.

Which was how Kat found herself waiting behind the red velvet curtain with five other women, all dressed as burlesque showgirls in flouncy, tightly corseted satin and lace dresses. Her hair was pinned up and elbow-length gloves graced her arms.

The group were gossiping idly, but sprang into life when the famous can-can music started up. All six grabbed their skirt hems and danced into the ring, their long legs kicking high.

There followed three minutes of frenzied dancing before a signal was given and they danced right back out again as quickly as they had arrived.

Kat, breathless but exhilarated, was last. She just made it out of the ring before she stumbled on shaky legs. Darrius, waiting for his cue to go back into the ring, only just caught her before she fell flat on her face.

'Sorry,' she gasped, mortified. 'I guess I'm not as fit as I thought I was.'

'Oh you look fit enough to me,' he murmured, slowly assessing her outfit. 'And it has to be said there's something so very primal about a woman throwing herself at a man's feet.'

With a smirk he continued on into the ring.

Ewww! What an ego! Kat had to resist the urge to wipe herself down.

'You'd better get some clothes on before you catch a chill,' barked Jake who had seen the exchange.

'Yes, sir,' she said smartly.

Then she left the tent with a smile on

her face and the key to Darrius' caravan hidden in her palm.

* * *

She'd left her phone in the pocket of a hoodie hanging on a hook and she grabbed it now. With the show still in full swing, there were few people about as she made her way to Darrius' caravan, ridiculously conscious of the loud swishing of her skirts. But she had to be back in the ring for another scene change before the interval, so there was no time to change.

Breaking the law did not come easy to Kat; somewhat ironic, considering she had been accused of doing exactly that. Picking pockets was a skill she had learned quite legitimately, as part of a magic act where her job had been sneaking marked playing cards into volunteers' pockets or removing wristwatches or other personal items that later magically turned up on stage in locked boxes.

But she was sweating, her hands slippery, as she tried to fit the key in the door. It turned smoothly and she was in.

The place was immaculately tidy. Either Darrius had some sort of compulsion, or he had something to hide. She smoothed her long gloves over her hands, and, using the torch on her phone, began her search without having the slightest idea what she was looking for.

The wardrobe contained trousers, shirts and jackets, a couple of pairs of shoes. She checked the pockets, tipped out the shoes. All empty.

Next the drawers, both in the bedroom and the kitchen. Again, nothing of interest. She was careful to leave everything exactly as she found it.

OK, so a next level search was required.

This involved checking the drawers again, this time for false bottoms or anything stuck underneath. Nothing.

The kitchen drawers and bathroom cabinet contained very few items, suggesting that Darrius didn't intend to be with the circus for long.

Mattress, pillows.

Fridge, toilet tank. Nothing.

She was pondering what to try next when her gaze fell on a mason jar of pasta on the kitchen counter. Her search had revealed no pots or pans, no jars of sauce. No veg in the fridge. Why would someone who clearly lived off takeaways have a jar of pasta?

Plunging her hand in, it only took her a moment to find a bank card. Dominic Brixton. Eureka! Aware that time was passing, she snapped a picture on her phone.

Resuming her search, she got lucky again with the kitchen bin. She'd already checked it and found it only had a few bits and bobs inside. But when she lifted it up to look underneath, it was noticeably heavier than it should be.

Lifting out the liner, she found a handgun in a plastic bag, taped securely to the bottom of the bin.

She sat down with a bump. What

would a man who dreamed of being a circus ringmaster need with a gun?

Kat turned the bag over in her hand, unsure what to do. The bank card had been a gift to her investigation, giving her something to work with, but the gun took things to a whole new level. Professionally she knew that it was virtually impossible to get a licence for a handgun in England so it was highly doubtful the gun was legal. But if she removed it, Darrius would know someone had been here.

On the other hand, it would be completely irresponsible to just leave it.

In the end she removed the bullets and put the gun back in the bag. The bullets, she stuffed deep inside one of her long gloves, lamenting the lack of decent hiding places in her saloon girl outfit.

Acutely aware that time was passing, she took another quick look around. And then another, more thorough look to make sure everything was exactly as she'd found it. Then she slipped out the door, making sure it locked behind her.

There was no time to dump the bullets. Picking her skirts up she hared back to the big top. The other dancers were just beginning to wonder where she had disappeared to when she ran up to join them, holding her phone between her teeth as she frantically tucked her hair back into some semblance of order. All the time she was acutely conscious of the weight of the bullets in her glove. Nellie was just coming out of the ring and Kat thrust her phone at her friend.

'Hold this for me, will you?'

And then they were in the ring and can-canning once more as the ring hands quickly picked up the pieces that had fallen off Noodle's ramshackle clown car, then threw fresh sawdust over the puddles of brightly coloured paint the clowns had splashed over the ring as part of their act.

Again, the dancers were only needed for a few minutes. Jake and a young Russian woman called Ivanna were waiting to go into the ring for an aerial silk act. He gave her a look as he passed but said nothing.

He would have to be told about the gun, she decided. The gun changed everything.

But first she had the problem of returning Darrius' key. And it had to be soon, in case he returned to his caravan during the interval.

Having introduced Jake and Ivanna, Darrius now stood at the side of the ring, watching the pair of them dangling from flimsy looking pieces of ribbon forty feet off the ground.

How to get the key back to him? Stumbling against him again was not an option. Nobody was that clumsy. Dropping it on the ground at his feet then 'finding' it for him was too obvious.

But time was moving on. She had to do something. Determinedly she took a step towards him but Noodle stepped in front of her.

'Give it to me,' he said quietly.

'What?' Kat feigned surprise.

'Whatever it was you took from him earlier.'

His tone brooked no argument. Kat handed it over. 'How did you know?'

'The real question is, how did everyone else not know? Dodn't you remember anything I told you?'

It was like being told off by a favourite teacher.

'I didn't have much time to plan!'

'That was always your problem, Kat. Too impulsive. And I'm not even going to ask what you were doing with it.' Palming the key, he started to walk towards Darrius.

'Wait,' she whispered. 'What will you do?'

'Watch me,' said Noodle and she did. The clown sauntered to the edge of the ring in his giant shoes, stopping right in front of Darrius, apparently too intent on observing the show to notice that he was blocking the ringmaster's view.

'Get out of the way.' Darrius gave him an impatient shove.

'Sorry,' said Noodle. Without looking

at Kat he gave her a subtle thumbs up.

He'd done it? Kat was in awe, glad she had never come up against him in a law enforcement capacity.

With that problem solved, she was debating whether or not to speak to Jake now or wait until he came home tonight.

Cheering and clapping from the ring made up her mind. Once more on terra firma, Jake and Ivanna were taking their bows. A second later they ran out while the ring hands went in to assemble the Wheel of Death.

Someone tossed him a towel and he wiped his face, swapping some words with Marty and Gary who were in their luminous skeleton outfits ready to enter the ring.

Kat stepped up to Jake.

'Can I have a quick word?'

Jake was dressed in a pair of silver leggings with an iridescent fish scale pattern to match Ivanna's mermaid costume. In the circus work, clothes were anything but modest and performers were so used to them they barely noticed. But Kat had been out of the circus for some time and faced with the stark reality of his broad, glistening chest she wondered if maybe she should have waited to speak to him.

'About what?' he asked, vigorously towelling his sweat-damp hair.

His bunched muscles appeared oiled under the lights, and Kat could feel the intense heat emanating from his skin.

'I . . .' She'd completely lost her train of thought.

At her stumbling silence Jake stopped and paid her more attention. His eyes narrowed.

'What have you done?' he asked her quietly.

Kat swallowed, still dazed by the vision of perfect masculinity.

'Er . . . maybe this isn't actually the best time . . .'

Jake caught her under the chin and tipped her head up, dragging her gaze away from his muscles and forcing her to meet his eye.

'Kat? Talk to me.'

People were looking at them. She

pulled herself together.

'Seriously. Not here. But it is important.' And she fled.

* * *

Jake watched her go. The coiling anxiety that had taken over his life told him he probably didn't want to know what she had been up to, but at the same time he couldn't stop looking at her. Had she any idea how beautiful she looked right now, cheeks glowing, blue eyes alight with excitement?

This was the Kat he had known, not the pale imitation who had returned to them. This was the woman he had missed —

'Are you ever going to tell her how you feel?' asked Noodle, dryly.

'I have no idea what you're talking about,' said Jake.

'Of course you don't.' Noodle turned serious. 'Maybe you needn't tell her how you feel about her, but you do have to tell her what's going on.'

'No,' said Jake.

'I don't see why not,' protested Noodle. 'She's one of us, Jake.'

Jake ran his hands through his hair.

'You saw her when she first arrived,' he said. 'She has troubles enough of her own. She doesn't need ours.'

'Maybe our troubles will take her mind off her own.'

'No,' said Jake firmly. 'Besides, it will be over soon,' he added with more confidence than he felt.

'You can't protect everyone, Jake. It's not your job.'

'Yes,' said Jake. 'It is.'

'I still think you're making a mistake,' said Noodle. 'She's changed. There's more to her than meets the eye.'

There always had been. Jake loved her complexity.

'You know what she's like,' he said. 'If we tell her, she'll go off half-cocked and do something stupid —' He broke off suddenly at Noodles expression. 'She's already done something, hasn't she?' he asked flatly.

Noodle swallowed.

'I think she's been in Bell's caravan.'

'She's done what?' roared Jake and everyone within earshot jumped.

Noodle told him everything.

The pounding in his temple suggested Jake's head might explode.

'I swear I'll kill her myself. OK,' he breathed. 'I'll speak to her. But in the meantime we have to ramp up our search.'

'How?' asked Noodle. 'We've been looking for days and not a sausage.'

'Then we need to try harder!'

A cry sounded from the ring, followed by a thud. Then shouts of alarm from the audience.

Jake, Noodle, everyone, immediately turned as one towards the curtain. Next moment they were running.

12

Back in the caravan, oblivious to the drama unfurling in the big top, Kat eagerly searched online for Dominic Brixton and found — nothing. No social media accounts — and if he'd ever been in any kind of trouble, it had never made it as far as the papers.

The lack of information was odd in itself; almost anyone these days typing in their name would be sure to find something.

She checked her watch. It wasn't too late, so she took out her phone and called her boss.

'Hi Paul, it's me again.'

'Hey.' He sounded pleased to hear from her. 'I was going to ring you. How's life on the road?'

She smiled. 'Better than you think.'

'I'll take your word for it. Did your pal turn up?'

'Not yet. I was wondering if you could

do me a favour?'

'Launder some money for you?'

She was silent.

'Sorry. Too soon?'

'You are an awful man, do you know that?'

'That's what my wife says.'

'Since you brought the case up, any news about the charges?'

'You know I can't talk about that,' he returned.

'I know.' She waited.

'Well, Nathan is toast,' said Paul cheerfully. 'Or he will be if we don't drop the ball. He has some fancy-schmancy lawyer who's going over everything we do with a fine tooth comb, so this conversation didn't happen, OK? I shouldn't tell you, but they found some encrypted files — in his laptop recycle bin. Presumably he thought he'd got rid of them.'

An image of the newspaper photo from the other day jumped into her mind and panic wound its way down her spine. She fought to keep her tone light.

'That sounds about right. He never

emptied a bin in his life.'

'Ooh, harsh. I'm not the only one with a warped sense of humour. Anyway, what are you ringing for? Need a bed again?'

'No, I'm sorted for a while. I even have a job.'

'In the circus? You always were a clown.'

'You're on a roll,' she said dryly. 'No. I . . . er . . . I wondered if you could look into someone for me?'

'Oh?'

It was just one word but she could feel his antennae shoot up.

'Look, kid, all joking aside, if this is to do with the investigation, then you had better keep your nose out of it. I mean that. So far they have nothing on you. Do not do anything that could be classed as interfering in an active investigation. Don't give them any ammo.'

'I promise it has nothing to do with the case,' she said quickly.

'OK then. Just so we're clear.'

'Can you find out anything about a man called Dominic Brixton?'

She could picture him searching for paper and a pen. 'In what context?'

'Anything. Does he have a record? Known alias, that sort of thing. In fact you could look for Darrius Bell as well.'

'Kid, you're worrying me.'

'He's someone here who may or may not be who he says he is, and may or may not be causing trouble for my friends.'

She couldn't mention the gun. Paul would bend the rules for her, but a gun was a whole different ball game. He'd be duty bound to act on that knowledge.

'Got that. How soon do you need it?'

She wanted to say right now. But apart from the bullets in her toilet bag, all she had on Darrius were suspicions and an innate dislike for the man.

'As soon as you can, please.' Something occurred to her. 'You were about to ring me?'

'Yeeaah.' He dragged the word out and now she was the one on alert.

'Paul?'

He took a deep breath.

'Nathan is out on bail. I thought you should know.'

* * *

When Jake finally returned to the caravan, Kat was sitting with her knees tucked up to her chin, deep in thought. What did Nathan's release mean for her? Nothing, hopefully. He of all people knew that she was ignorant of his criminal activity.

So why had he sent that man to intimidate her?

It didn't matter. Even if he wanted to speak to her, he had no idea where she was. She was safe here, safe to pursue her own investigation into Darrius.

When Jake came in, she put all thoughts of Nathan aside, eager to fill him in with this evening's activities and show him the proof that Darrius was up to no good. But one glance at his face blew everything else from her mind. He had that drawn look that only came with bad news.

'What is it? What's happened?' she demanded.

'Everyone's fine,' he said quickly.

'But?'

'There was an accident.'

She felt the colour draining from her face.

'Tell me.'

'Gary, Marty's brother, had a fall . . .'

Kat knew who the Allen brothers were. And she knew their act. She could barely get the words out.

'A fall from the Wheel of Death?'

Jake clearly knew what she was thinking.

'It's not the same as your parents,' he hurried to reassure her. 'Marty and Gary had barely started their act. There was no speed, no real height. He just got his timing wrong and slipped. He says it looked worse than it was. And he managed to get to his feet and convince the audience it was all part of the act.'

'He slipped,' she repeated, ice sliding through her veins.

'A minor slip,' stressed Jake. 'Not from

the top or anything. I mean, he's fine and wanted to continue, but I made him see a medic just in case.'

'A minor slip,' she echoed. She had begun to shake. Jake took an anxious step towards her but she held up a hand stopping him in his tracks.

'It's OK, Kat,' he said gently in a tone he might have used to soothe one of the horses. 'I mean it. Everyone's fine.'

She wrapped her arms around herself and closed her eyes, his news too tangled up with heartache and pain for her to process.

'Everyone's fine? Well that's OK, then, isn't it? Did you cancel the act?'

'What? No, of course not!'

Her eyes flew open.

'Of course not. Tell me, who stepped in?'

'I did.'

A numbness was spreading over her limbs. She nodded, knowing she had expected no less. The great, the invincible Jake Romero to the rescue.

'He could have died,' she said, her

voice rising.

'But he didn't.' Again he half reached out to her and again she pulled away.

'He has a new baby,' she continued. 'A baby that could have grown up without a father.'

'I know. He claims that's what went wrong. Lack of sleep. He says his concentration was shot.'

Still hugging herself she began to rock.

'This is your fault,' she whispered.

Jake flinched and sat down suddenly, as if his legs wouldn't hold him. He rubbed a hand over his jaw, his beard making a rasping sound. He looked absolutely shattered and she didn't care.

'Do you think I don't know that?' he said, his voice cracking. 'Of course he's not getting enough sleep with a new baby. I should have been more aware and checked on him.'

'No,' she lashed out. 'It's your fault because you allow that act to continue when you know how dangerous it is. Just because it pulls the crowds in. You could have put a stop to it long ago.' She heard her voice rising but was helpless to control it, or the tears streaming down her face. 'What is wrong with you people? Do you never think of the consequences, the lives that could be ruined . . .'

Jake said nothing, refusing to defend himself because, of course, he had no defence.

'How can you?' she continued, building up a head of steam. 'How can you just carry on?'

'Nothing did happen.'

'But it nearly did! There has to be a better way to make a living!'

* * *

Walking back to the caravan to break the news to Kat, Jake had known it would come to this. They both knew this was no longer about Gary. This was an old argument, repeated almost daily for months before nineteen-year-old Kat had finally packed her bags and left, claiming she couldn't live like this any more.

It was an argument about safety, and risk, and lifestyle choices. An argument Jake could end right here and now simply by telling her the truth about her parents' accident.

But now, as then, he couldn't do that to her.

'Say something,' she insisted.

'Whatever I say will only make it worse. And you're upset enough,' he said wearily. 'But you're wrong, Kat. There is no better way to make a living. Not for Gary, not for me, nor for anyone else here. This is the life we've chosen.'

'But it doesn't have to be like this,' she insisted. 'There are other jobs.'

It had been a long day. A long week, if he was honest. Jake's temper flared.

'Working in a factory? Driving a bus? Here we're at the top of our game. Gary and Marty are legends. They could work anywhere in the world.'

'But —'

'Then there's Noodle. Who would give him a job if his shady past came out? And me, Kat? What would I do?'

'You have skills —'

'Skills that are honed to perfectly suit the world I live in. Could you see me in an office?'

She faltered. 'Dyslexia isn't the problem it used to be. There's help . . .'

'Here I don't need help. I know my job inside out.'

'You could work with animals.'

'Not well paying and I'd need qualifications.'

'Farming, then.'

'Listen to yourself.' He threw up his hands. 'Where would I get the money to buy a farm? Oh, I see. You mean I could labour for someone else? Thanks. Or I could stay here, continue to be my own boss and do a job I love.'

He reined himself in. Kat was hurting. He knew that, but they had been over this too many times for him just to take it lying down.

'You just don't see the alternatives because you don't want to.'

He pinched the bridge of his nose and dug deep to find some patience.

'So everyone on the outside has perfect lives? They don't have problems?' he countered, his annoyance winning out. 'Bills? Mortgages? Getting their kids into the right schools?'

'They don't risk their lives every day.'

'Sure they do, getting in a car or a plane.'

'That's different.'

He'd had enough. 'Tell me, then. If life on the outside is so brilliant, why are you here?'

Wariness entered her expression. 'To visit Delilah.'

'So you say. But why now, after all this time?'

'Why would you ask me that?'

'Why? Let me see.' He counted off the reasons on his fingers. 'Your clothes are good quality but you don't have many of them, as if you packed in a hurry. You yourself admitted that you have no roof over your head, but clearly you haven't been living on the streets. I know you paid for supplies in town the other day when Nellie forgot the bank card, so you're not short of money. You do seem to be short of friends, though. And no ring on your finger.'

All colour had drained from her face. 'What do you mean?'

'Delilah told me you were engaged.'

He waited to see what she had to say; he'd had many a sleepless night over this one.

Defiant blue eyes told him to mind his own business.

'It . . . it didn't work out.'

'Sorry to hear that. But as I may have mentioned before, life doesn't always run smoothly, wherever you live, however you make a living.'

'That's different. The circus is just dangerous —'

'No it's not,' he said, exasperated. 'I've said time and time again that every risk we take is calculated. No one here has a death wish. Everyone loves their family. If we aren't a hundred percent confident in what we are doing, we don't do it. Whether it suits your view of the world or not, we're doing fine. Living life our way.'

He'd gone too far. Turquoise flames sparked in her eyes as they always had when she felt attacked.

'Are you, Jake? Living life your way? Because if you ask me, you're living more Darrius Bell's way, jumping when he says jump.'

He gritted his teeth.

'Is that why you searched his caravan?'

She stared back, eyes as stormy as the ocean.

'How did you . . . Of course. Noodle.'

'And what did you find?'

She tossed her head.

'A gun.'

'What the — ?' Jake exploded out of his seat.

'I told you. I found a gun. So, does Darrius bother you now? Are you concerned about Delilah now?'

'I was always concerned about her.'

'Are you? Because it doesn't really feel like that to me. In fact maybe we should try and call her right now? And maybe I'll contact the police if she doesn't answer. How does that sound?'

'You can't call the police,' he said desperately

'Watch me,' she said. 'I'll try Delilah first.'

She dialled.

And a phone began to ring in Jake's bedroom.

13

They both froze, staring at each other, Kat in confusion, Jake in horror.

Next minute, she dived for the bedroom door. So did Jake. He got there first.

'Get out of my way,' she snarled and he did so, hands held up in a gesture of surrender.

She found Delilah's candy-pink phone in his bedside drawer. Her hand shook as she lifted it out. In fact she was shaking all over with panic, with fear, with confusion.

Jake filled the doorway. There was no way past him. She looked around frantically for a weapon. Finding none she rolled swiftly across the bed, putting it between the pair of them.

She didn't take her eyes off him as she stuffed Delilah's phone into the pocket of her hoodie and dialled on her own phone. She held it up to show him two nines, her thumb hovering over the third.

'Tell me right now what you've done with her.'

'Kat, look, I can explain —'

'You have ten seconds.'

'Please, Kat.' His green eyes were pleading.

'Nine.'

'Kat, I'm begging you.'

That stopped her. Jake Romero begging?

'Then tell me.'

'Let me get the others,' he said, sounding defeated.

'What others?'

She was suspicious of everything he said now. Jake of all people was responsible for Delilah's disappearance? That made no sense.

'Noodle. Marty. Xerxes. I'll get them. Promise me you won't do anything until I get back.'

They were all involved? Her confusion climbed to a whole new level.

'Why should I promise you anything?'

'Kat. Please.' There was a helplessness

in his tone that suddenly made her very afraid. Not for herself, but for Delilah.

'You have ten minutes.'

* * *

It took less than that. Noodle, Nellie, Xerxes, Marty, Phaedra and a few others filed in silently. Soon there was standing room only. Someone drew the curtains. Phaedra went out to stand watch.

Some looked frightened. Some looked relieved.

'So what's made you all lie to me?' she asked boldly, though she felt unimaginably nervous.

'Delilah's been kidnapped,' said Jake flatly.

'That's not funny,' said Kat.

'He's serious,' said Nellie. 'Delilah's in trouble, love. We all are. We've been struggling to know what to do.'

'How can she have been kidnapped? I mean, by whom?'

Normal people didn't just get kidnapped. And neither Delilah's family nor the circus had any money, so who would pay for her release?

Glances were exchanged. Feet were shuffled. No one spoke up so she rounded on Jake.

'Tell me.'

'Four days ago I had a call from Darrius Bell,' he began. 'He had a proposition for me, something that would be of financial benefit to the circus. And to him, of course. I've met his type before and they're almost always dodgy, so I said I wasn't interested and hung up.

'But Delilah was here and listening in. She wanted to hear him out. You know what she's like — she started getting giddy about what we could buy; new acts, new equipment. Even a new tent. She wouldn't shut up.'

Kat did know what she was like; bubbly and positive. Delilah would have been sure Darrius' intentions were pure.

'She reminded me revenues were down and money was tight. She persuaded me there was no harm in just listening to him. So I called him back and arranged to meet. Anyway, he showed up after the evening performance.'

Jake went silent. You could hear a pin drop.

'I didn't like the look of him from the start but I'd promised to listen to him so I did.'

'What did he want?'

'To be honest, I didn't even let him get that far at that point. He was so confident that he 'knew what circus people were like' and began laying down the law about how we had to remember he was in charge and we'd have to follow his orders.

'Well, he soon found out exactly what circus people were like.' He gave a tiny smile. 'By then even Delilah had figured out that he was up to no good. She was gutted to see all her big plans fly out the window and she gave him what for. I mean, she really let rip. He didn't like being spoken to like that but then we didn't like the way he had spoken to us, either. Xerxes here showed him the door.'

Kat waited, bursting with questions but with enough sense to keep them to herself for now.

'The following day Delilah didn't turn up for the matinee.'

'Wait? That was Wednesday?' said Kat. 'I spoke to her that morning and she invited me here. She told me something good was happening. She sounded really excited. I thought she meant —' She broke off.

'What?'

'Never mind. Go on,' she said.

'I didn't know she'd spoken to you at that point. But she didn't turn up for the evening performance either, which wasn't like her. Ivanna covered but we were worried, especially when she didn't answer her phone.

'We knew she'd gone to the supermarket so after the show Marty and I drove there. We found her car with a load of food defrosting in the boot. She must have been snatched while loading up —'

He paused before gathering himself.

'Darrius must have been waiting and

watching. He rang her phone, which we found in the car. He wanted another meeting. And he hoped I'd be more reasonable this time.'

'He took her,' said Kat,' her mouth dry as she tried not to think of Delilah's confusion and fear. 'What does he want?'

'That's easy. He wants us to steal the Tintoretto.'

She looked at everyone. Her fear mirrored theirs.

'Or?'

'She dies.'

The silence in the crowded caravan was total.

Kat thought of Darrius, his steely eyes. His weird presence. And she knew they believed him.

She did, too.

She worked it out.

'So she'd been gone twenty-four hours when I turned up?'

No wonder everyone had been so nervous.

'We tried to make you leave,' said Nellie, reaching for her hand. 'We didn't want to but we couldn't risk putting anyone else in danger. We didn't know what else to do.'

Kat looked at Jake.

'Do you know where they are holding her?'

'Not yet.'

Jake was tight-lipped. She nodded. Of course they had been looking for her. She would expect no less.

'But you know she's alive?' She braced herself for the answer.

'Yes. We insisted on that. We get one call a day but it's only a few seconds. She's never been able to pass on a message.'

'And you haven't called the police.'

It was a statement; obviously they hadn't.

'Since when have they ever cared about us?' mumbled Xerxes.

She nodded again. The police would have to work within the rules, whereas everyone here would do what they had to, to get one of their own back.

Including her, she realised. This

wasn't the time to tell them she was a police officer. They might not believe she would do whatever it took.

'What are his plans for the painting? How on earth are we supposed to steal it?'

She saw them register the 'we,' and the entire room collectively relaxed.

'He's left that up to us,' said Jake dryly. 'Apparently 'people like us' have a special gift for larceny. But the painting is why he was so pleased to learn who you are. He's done his research. He hopes to use you as a way into the Hall. In fact he's been angling for me to get you on board for days.'

'Oh, he has?'

Her mind was racing. No way was she stealing from Lord H . . . but she might have to play along to buy them some time.

'We're only here another five days?' Everyone nodded. 'So that gives us our timescale. And you've been looking for Delilah, I presume?'

'Ever since they took her,' said Jake.

'Darrius never leaves the circus. Finn and Dmitri come and go and we've followed them every time — not easy as they know most of us, and some of us stick out like a sore thumb.' He looked at Noodle, as always in costume, and Xerxes who was six foot six and built like Bluto from *Popeye*.

'We've had the ring hands do it. They don't know why they're following them but since both Finn and Dmitri are lazy so-and-sos, they're happy to report back anything that might get them into trouble. So far, though, they just seem to be running errands.'

Kat considered what they had.

'Can you get a list of where they go? They might be passing messages on or getting information.'

Jake nodded. 'Sure.'

'Do their cars have GPS?' she continued.

Everyone looked at each other.

'Not that we know of.'

'Can someone check that out? We might be able to find out where they went on the day she disappeared. And what about their mobiles? It's a long shot, but if we had the chance we could check locations for the days leading up to the kidnapping. Or maybe put a tracking app on their phones . . .'

They were all looking at her.

'Sorry,' she mumbled. 'You'll have thought of all of that.'

'No. We didn't think of any of those things. And they're good ideas. Marty, you can get into their cars, can't you?' said Jake.

Marty adopted a look of innocence.

'For the record, I have no idea what you are talking about, but yes, I can.'

Jake flashed a quick smile.

'And Noodle, can I leave the phones to you?'

The clown nodded. 'They never have them out of their hands, though, so it won't be easy. And I don't even know what you mean by checking location, so someone else will have to do that.'

'Great,' said Kat. 'And I have this.' She showed them the snap of Dominic

Brixton's bank card. 'Alias Darrius Bell.'

Excited chatter ensued.

'But how . . .'

'She broke into his caravan,' said Jake, dryly.

Several people smiled.

'Attagirl,' beamed Nellie.

'So far it's not been much of a help,' admitted Kat. 'I found nothing on social media for either name. I've asked a friend to look into it but it could be a while before he gets back to me.'

'Our Tom could do that,' said Nellie. 'My nephew,' she explained to Kat. 'He's studying computers at college.'

The nephew who hoped to be a clown, Kat remembered.

'I don't want him doing anything illegal.'

'Neither do I,' said Nellie and winked.

Everyone looked at each other. The atmosphere was less hopeless now that they had things to do.

Soon everyone left, silently. As she closed the caravan door, Kat turned to see Jake studying her.

'Where did you learn about all that?' he asked. 'GPS. Taking charge.'

Oops. It was pretty standard stuff for the start of an investigation.

'It's all out there,' she hedged. 'The internet is a great resource.'

'I'm sure it is.' He was still staring. Then his shoulders relaxed. 'I'm sorry. Clearly everyone was right. I should have told you sooner.'

Kat could now understand the stress he'd been under. For someone in his charge to be placed in danger was devastating for a man like Jake. How much worse if it was the woman he loved?

'We'll find her,' she said softly.

He nodded. 'We will.'

'You should get some sleep,' she said.

'I will.' He remained sitting, staring at the floor.

Kat sensed his despair and wanted nothing more than to enfold him in her arms. But she reminded herself that hers weren't the arms he wanted.

Going into her room, she closed the door.

14

Next day, it felt as if a cloud had been lifted over Circus Mara. The danger was still very real but people were more cheerful as they went about their day.

Kat noticed, and knew that if she had, Darrius would too. She'd mention it later when they gathered again to share their progress.

Since nothing could happen until they found Delilah, the show had to go on. Kat spent the morning training with Xerxes, tied to a spinning board painted to look like a target, while he threw innumerable knives at her, outlining the shape of her body.

There were a good many people around; practising, moving equipment, talking, laughing. Kat knew that rehearsing like this was the only way to go — there would be a lot of distraction during a show. Her job would be far more nerve-racking if Xerxes could only work in total silence.

'You did good,' he beamed, slapping a shovel-like hand on her shoulder. 'Tell me what kind of job you could you do on the outside that would give you that thrill?'

Policing had given her a thrill. Until it had all gone horribly wrong.

'Some folk get a thrill from baking a cake,' she joked, pretending to check her clothes for holes.

'But not you,' said Xerxes confidently. 'This is where you belong, Kat. With us. How do you feel about being in the show this afternoon? I mean, you barely flinched.' His booming laugh rang out.

'Do you mean it?' she said, pleased with his vote of confidence. 'Great! I'll have a word with Nellie and sort out an outfit.'

She didn't find Nellie but she did find Jake outside Gary Allen's caravan. Gary was there too, holding the new baby. His other child, a little girl of about three, was standing on Jake's shoulders, arms outstretched, being zoomed around in circles.

Jake had a firm grip on the child's waist and her laughter filled the air.

Kat stilled as she watched them, her heart clenching with emotion. Jake looked so natural. He'd make a great father. If they had stayed together, this could be their mop-haired little girl.

If only they had made different choices.

If only. The saddest words in any language.

'I'm an aeroplane!' the child shrieked. 'And I'm a giant.'

'A giant aeroplane?' Jake suggested.

'No. Do giant steps,' she ordered and Jake obliged, taking huge steps.

'Fe fi fo fum,' he intoned. 'I spy . . . Kat? Come and meet Maddie. Maddie, tell Kat who this is.'

'Thomas,' said Maddie in disgust. 'He's a baby. He can't even talk. All he can do is this.' She filled her lungs and screamed at the top of her voice.

'Shh,' begged her father with a panicked look at the baby. 'Sibling rivalry didn't take long to rear its ugly head,' he said ruefully. 'Listen, Kat, I hear you were upset about my accident. Just want you to know I'm OK.'

She tensed and glanced at Jake, realising that he was probably here to check up on Gary.

Gary intercepted the look.

'It was my fault entirely,' he continued. 'And a valuable lesson. I'll never get in the ring again without double-checking that I'm in a fit state. Not when I have so much to lose.' He kissed his baby's head.

Maddie started wriggling to get down. 'I want to see the goats.'

'Why don't I take her?' suggested Jake and Gary nodded in relief.

'Kat?' asked Jake. 'Fancy a walk?'

She nodded. 'Do you know where the goats are, Maddie?'

'Mhmm.' Maddie began to march on stocky legs and they followed.

The child knew everyone and everyone knew her. She stopped to talk or stroke a dog, always chattering. She reminded Kat of herself at that age and the unique freedom she'd had, being raised on a circus.

When they reached the goat pen Maddie dropped to her knees with complete disregard for her clothes and began tearing up daises to feed to the goats, who were obviously old friends.

'She's so cute,' said Kat with a longing she had never been aware of before.

'She's a firebrand,' agreed Jake fondly. 'How are you getting on with the goat training?'

'They are hell's own imps,' she said. 'But great fun. We're reaching an understanding.'

The goats were leaping in their pen and Maddie, started to throw herself about madly, copying them.

'I can jump higher,' she said.

'I can see that,' said Jake.

'Will you and Delilah will ever have kids?' Kat blurted. They would make beautiful children.

He turned to her in surprise.

'Me and Delilah? Why on earth would you say that?'

'Well, because you're a couple. Aren't you?'

'No.' The word held total bewilderment.

'But I thought . . . I mean, her clothes were in your caravan. I assumed . . .'

'I cleared her caravan because Finn and Dmitri were moving in to it. Can you imagine her reaction if she thought they'd been through her stuff?'

Kat could indeed. She felt foolish, but also more than a little bit pleased.

Jake turned to her and took a deep breath.

'Just so we are clear, there is nothing between me and Delilah. Never has been, never could be.' His voice had a strange timbre to it, thick with things unspoken.

Kat's heart rate picked up. She had to ask.

'Why never?'

At first she thought he wasn't going to answer. But then he gave a helpless shrug.

'Because this,' he said hoarsely, and kissed her.

Lightning. It was the only way to describe the touch of his lips on hers. Kat's breathing and heartbeat stopped. She was still reeling when he drew back.

'I should probably have asked about your engagement before I did that.'

'Off,' said Kat, rising onto her toes to return his kiss. 'Definitely off. And there's no one else.'

Had she ever been kissed like this before? Maybe ten years ago, but not since. Why, oh why had she given this up?

A tiny thunderbolt rammed into her legs.

'My Jake!' said Maddie tearfully, holding up her arms to be lifted.

He picked her up and the little girl covered his face with sloppy kisses. 'See,' said Maddie.

'I do see,' said Jake. 'Sorry,' he mouthed to Kat.

'A worthy opponent,' grinned Kat. It was wonderful to see how patient he was with the toddler whose world had been turned upside down by the new arrival.

'Would you like to help me train the goats, Maddie?'

The child considered. 'And wear sparkles in the ring?'

Kat had made an occasional appearance in the ring when she was younger than Maddie. But that was a decision for her parents. She looked to Jake.

'When your mummy and daddy say you can. But for now you can help Kat teach them how to jump.'

'I can.' Maddie nodded vigorously. 'I'm good at jumping.'

'That you are,' said Jake. 'I'd better take her back,' he told Kat, flashing her a smile. 'God, I've missed you. I can't believe I had the courage to finally do that.'

'And I can't believe that it took you so long.'

'Can we continue this later?'

'And by 'this' you mean more kissing?'

'I certainly do mean that.'

'Then yes,' she said happily.

He swung Maddie onto his shoulders and sauntered off, walking backwards so he could continue to keep Kat in his sights.

Nellie was walking past, carrying a basket of costumes. She looked from Jake to Kat, took in their stupid grins and rolled her eyes.

'Well I'm glad that's finally sorted,' she said with satisfaction.

Kat took one handle of the basket and began walking with her.

'I don't know what you mean,' she said but couldn't wipe the smile off her face.

Nellie dug a teasing elbow into her ribs.

'Yes you do. A blind donkey could see the way you two have been sidling around each other. Anyway, I'm right glad everything is out in the open now. I hate secrets.'

Kat felt a twinge of guilt. Should she come clean about her job? But she still wasn't sure how people would take it if she told them. Would they close her out again, even unconsciously? No; she needed to be involved, needed to be here for Delilah.

'I'm taking Hazel's place in Xerxes' act this afternoon,' she said. 'I need a costume.'

It was the perfect thing to say to distract Nellie.

'Oh! I have the very thing. You'll wow them!'

* * *

Half an hour later Kat was self-consciously clad in a belly dancer outfit, jewels studding the waistband and cuffs of graceful harem pants and her bra.

'You look perfect,' said Nellie, stepping back to admire her handiwork. 'I've had this one for a while but I needed someone with just the right figure. If Xerxes wasn't a happily married man, I'd be worried he'd be too distracted to aim straight.'

Kat tugged at the bra.

'I feel a bit exposed,' she admitted. It was a while since she'd appeared in public wearing so little. In Mauritius with Nathan, if she was correct.

'Well, as I say, you have the figure for it. Now what about your hair? I'm thinking pile it high and dot it with more jewels. The audience will love it when he pretends to slip and hits your hair.'

'Can I have pretend hair too, in that case?' asked Kat, picturing herself with lopsided locks.

'Easy,' said Nellie, rifling in a bag of wigs. 'In fact it'll be great if they think he's chopped it off!'

Kat sat down in front of a mirror while Nellie began to experiment with her hair.

'Aren't you scared?' Nellie asked. 'I mean, whatever job you did on the outside, I doubt you'd have had knives thrown at you?'

Don't be so sure, thought Kat. Police work had its moments. She tamped down another twinge of guilt and made light of Nellie's comment.

'Let's face it, if Xerxes makes a mistake I won't be in any position to worry. Besides, he has a perfect safety record.'

'I know. But I also know you think a lot of what we do is dangerous,' said

Nellie casually.

'I absolutely wouldn't do it if I didn't trust Xerxes one hundred percent.'

In the mirror Nellie met and held her eye.

'I get it,' said Kat quietly. And she did. Calculated risk, just as Jake always said. And Gary had said he'd learned a lesson last night. But she wasn't ready to give up her argument.

'I know everyone here is confident in their skills but so were my parents. Accidents can happen.'

'They can,' agreed Nellie. 'It's all about trust and personal responsibility. Like you and Xerxes.'

'But some things are riskier than others. You have to admit that.'

'Riskier than knives?' asked Nellie dryly.

'OK, it's the Wheel of Death. I can't bear to think about it. The thought of it destroying any more lives keeps me awake at night.'

'I know love.' Nellie gently rested her hands on Kat's shoulders and looked at her in the mirror. 'And everyone understands.' She hesitated.

'What is it?' asked Kat.

Nellie appeared to make up her mind.

'There's something you need to know, Kat. About Dan and Mara's accident that day.'

Kat frowned. 'What do you mean?'

Nellie's eyes were full of sympathy.

'I think it would be better coming from Jake, love. Ask him.'

15

It was a long time since Jake had felt this good. Of course he was still worried to death about Delilah, but he couldn't get that kiss with Kat out of his head. It had been a long time coming and he was looking forward to many more in the near future.

In fact, talk of the devil, here she was now coming towards him — and man, what a costume. He swung between open admiration for her taut figure and jealousy that so many other men were craning their necks to watch her go by.

He knew he had a big soppy grin on his face when she reached him, but was helpless to hide it.

'When we arranged to pick up where we left off, I didn't expect you to dress for the occasion,' he teased.

'Tell me about my parents,' she said and just like that, Jake's goofy smile faded.

'What?' he asked, stupidly.

'There's some big secret,' she said. 'I want to know what.'

Jake's chest contracted.

'W . . . who told you?'

'Does it matter?' There was stubbornness and determination in her eyes, but also tension. She was braced for something bad. 'Tell me.'

Jake had always known this moment would come. That it had come now, when they'd briefly found each other again, was just bad luck.

He took her hand.

'Not here.'

She didn't resist as he led her to the office, but she was shivering as he sat her in the only chair. 'You're cold. Let me get you something —'

'Just tell me, Jake!'

He swallowed, knowing there was no way to sugar coat this.

'Your father was drinking on the night of the accident.'

'Liar,' she spat immediately, and he flinched.

'It's true. I'm sorry. Your father had a problem.'

'I refuse to listen to this.' She leapt to her feet.

Helpless, Jake made no move to stop her. But she stopped herself at the door.

'Why would you even say that?' she asked, still with her back to him.

'Come and sit down,' he urged. 'Please.'

She shook him off angrily, but did as he suggested, sitting with her arms folded, refusing to look at him.

'Why would you of all people spread lies like that? I thought you loved my father!'

'I did. But it is true, Kat. Sometimes he drank too much.'

'No.'

Now Jake had started, he had to see it through.

'It was the worst kept secret on the circus. If he hadn't been in charge, he'd have been given his marching orders long before.'

'No,' she repeated stubbornly. 'He

would never do that. He would never take those kinds of risks.'

'Why do you think your mother was performing the Wheel of Death with him that night?' asked Jake, gently. 'It was his and Kevin's act but Kevin refused to work with him again until he got help. The Wheel had been retired for weeks because no one trusted him.'

'That's not true.' She continued to shake her head. 'The enquiry said it was an accident.'

'No,' said Jake, sadly. 'That's just what we told you. He'd been off the drink for a while and seemed to be doing well. But Kevin was away that night and for some reason your dad decided to resurrect the act. Revenues were down and maybe he felt we needed a boost. Who knows.'

She continued to stare at the floor.

'No one would partner with him but he was the boss, so they couldn't stop him either. He had a drink before going into the ring that night.'

'No. Not true.'

'I'm sorry, Kat, but I saw him,' said

Jake. 'He had a little silver hip flask.'

Her head shot up. Was that a glimmer of recognition in her eyes? If so, it was instantly wiped out by a look of sheer disbelief.

'You saw him drinking and didn't stop him?'

Jake had no defence. He had to see this through even though he knew it would probably destroy any chance he and Kat might have of a relationship.

'I was fifteen and into physical fitness. I'd never had a drink so I had no idea what it could do to a person's judgment. And as I said, he was the boss.

'I told your mum what I'd seen. She said it would be fine and not to tell anyone else. So I didn't. And I've been sorry every single day of my life since.'

'No,' Kat kept shaking her head. 'None of this is true. The wheel is lethal. Everyone knows that.'

'He wasn't obviously drunk,' Jake continued. 'No one would have allowed that. Misadventure, they called it. An error of judgment. I'm sorry.'

Kat stood up and walked out of the door without looking back.

* * *

Kat went straight to Jake's caravan since she had no space of her own. She threw herself on her bed, pummelling the pillow until her arms ached.

How dare he! How dare he say those horrible things about her parents!

When she could pummel no more she buried her face in the battered pillow and sobbed until she had run out of tears. That took a long time. She'd missed the afternoon show and was sorry, but no way was she ready to face anyone right now.

Eventually her tears dried up and her emotions drained away, leaving her able to think more clearly.

She recognised the flask Jake had described; her father kept it in the glove box of his car and simply tapped the side of his nose when she'd asked him about it.

Plus, her mother, although a talented artiste in her own right had been totally in thrall of her dad, always backing his grandiose ideas.

Could what Jake said be true? Were they responsible for their own accident — her dad through recklessness, her mum through misplaced loyalty?

Twice someone came and tapped on her door but, too wrapped up in her misery, she ignored them. Even when the matinee was over, she simply could not rouse herself.

Everyone must have known about this. So everyone was part of the cover-up.

No, not a cover-up, she told herself. She had been fourteen at the time of the accident and had just lost both her parents. People had simply protected her as best they could.

And the results of the inquest were out there. Why had she never looked them up? Because she had always suspected something wasn't right?

Finally, she fell into an exhausted sleep. It was dark outside when she finally stirred. She showered and dressed in jeans and T-shirt, leaving her long hair to dry naturally. Her pillow was covered in stage make-up and tears, and probably beyond saving.

Checking her watch she realised she had missed the evening show, too, and owed Xerxes an apology. Jake, too. He hadn't deserved to shoulder this burden for so long. None of them did.

The show was over, but everyone planned to gather and report any progress in the search for Delilah. Kat made her way to the big top. Since the truth seemed to be coming out right left and centre, maybe it was time for her to come clean about her job as a police officer.

Everyone was in the tent, just as she'd expected. They grew quiet as she pushed past the flap and she knew they had been talking about her.

'Are you OK, love?' asked Nellie.

'I'm fine.' Which was maybe a bit optimistic, but she would be. 'I'm sorry for letting you down today,' she told Xerxes. 'It won't happen again.'

'No problem, Kat.'

Jake stood there, pale and silent and she was sorry she had added to his stress when things were already so difficult. He, too, deserved an apology, but this wasn't the time or place, so she went to his side, sliding her hand into his. She felt his initial surprise then to her immense relief he squeezed her hand and locked his fingers tightly around hers.

'So,' Jake said taking the lead. 'Do we have anything to report?'

'Neither Dmitri nor Finn went anywhere today so that's a big fat zilch,' said Marty, glumly. 'Plus there's no sat nav in either car.'

'I managed to get hold of Finn's phone,' reported Noodle. 'Short of chopping off his finger, no one is going to get into it.'

'Our Tom did manage to find something on Dominic Brixton,' piped up Nellie. 'He's been in court a few times for petty stuff when he was younger, but nothing recent.'

Or he had just grown better at not getting

caught, thought Kat with her professional hat on.

'Kat, have you heard from your friend?' asked Marty.

'Not yet. I'll chase it up tomorrow if we don't —'

The curtains parted and Darrius, Finn and Dmitri walked in.

* * *

'A social gathering, Jacob? You didn't invite me.'

'This is circus business, Darrius. It doesn't concern you.'

'Well I, too, have circus business to discuss, so I'll wait if you don't mind.' His cool grey eyes took in everyone present, lingering a little too long on Kat. 'Don't let me interrupt,' he added when no one spoke.

'Actually, we're done now,' said Jake.

'Then may I?' said Darrius. 'Someone has been in my caravan. And I would like to know who.'

He was still looking directly at Kat.

'That's crazy,' said Jake, immediately. 'No one here would do that.'

'Let's just skip past all the denials shall we?' said Darrius. 'Because someone did., Was it you, Ms Turnado? You do have a bit of a reputation for sneaking around, don't you?'

Jake stepped in front of her.

'Listen, Darrius,' he began.

Dmitri and Finn made a move towards him. Xerxes and Marty both moved too and Kat made a quick decision before everything got out of hand.

'Yes, it was me,' she said, pushing past Jake. 'But only because you kidnapped my friend.'

The temperature dropped at least ten degrees and everyone held their breath. Jake was once more by her side and she could feel his tension.

Darius looked at Jake.

'She knows? Oh, this is most unfortunate, Jacob. Most unfortunate indeed.'

'She hasn't told anyone,' said Jake quickly.

'I'm afraid I don't have the same trust

in her that you do.'

'So you're not denying it?' demanded Kat.

'Kat,' warned Jake.

'Hush, Jacob. This is now between me and Ms Turnado. No, I'm not denying it. I really had no choice when your friends here were so uncooperative.'

'You'll never get away with it,' snarled Kat.

Darrius' chuckle sounded almost genuine.

'Such a cliché, Ms Turnado. I'd have hoped for something more original. Dmitri? Would you go outside and make sure no one else is lurking?'

Once he'd gone, Darrius drew the pistol out of his pocket. There were gasps of shock from everyone except Kat and Jake.

Kat stared at the weapon. She reckoned that with her training, and at this distance, she could disarm him, especially as she knew the gun wasn't loaded. There were enough people here to physically overpower Darrius and Finn.

But what would happen to Delilah then?

Darrius seemed amused by her indecision.

'I see you recognise this, Ms Turnado. Just to let you know that it is once again locked and loaded.'

Kat's mind raced. That the gun was loaded changed everything. Any shot in such an enclosed space could do serious damage.

'Where are you holding Delilah?' she said, knowing she'd get no answer, but needing time to think. Though to be honest, she was all out of options.

'You'll find out soon enough when you join her.'

'Over my dead body —' snarled Jake.

'Calm yourself, Romero,' snapped Darrius. 'Have we harmed anyone yet? I'm sure the Delectable Delilah will be delighted to have company. They can do each other's nails.'

'She's going nowhere,' said Jake. 'We need her in the show, and besides, Lord Huntersly will notice her absence.'

'Ah, good point. That's why I keep you around. In that case, what are we going to do with you, Ms Turnado? I suppose you could move in with Finn and Dmitri to watch over you? I do feel you and Finn have some sort of rapport.'

'Not going to happen,' grated Jake.

Kat felt panic rising. She couldn't be locked up! How would she help find Delilah then? She had to convince Darrius that she wasn't a threat, so she blurted the first thing that came into her head.

'I could be useful.'

Even as she said it an idea began to form. She wished she had time to warn the others but she could only hope and pray they would play along.

'I've known for a while now what was going on, and I haven't told a soul.' She took a deep breath. 'I think we can help each other.'

Darrius cocked his head.

'I'd like to trust you, Ms Turnado, I really would.'

'Then make me an offer.'

'What?' Darrius frowned.

She'd surprised him. She pressed the advantage.

'Yes, we want Delilah back safe — that's non-negotiable. But when you first made contact with Jake, you said stealing the painting could be to our mutual benefit. So make it worth our while to really throw in with you, rather than working against you.'

She could feel the buzz of shock in everyone around her. Nellie gasped and Jake recoiled. Kat didn't dare look at anyone.

'Well, well. This is unexpected,' said Darrius.

Dmitri burst in. 'Boss!'

'Not now,' snapped Darrius.

'But boss. The police are here.'

Darrius moved like lightning. He thrust the gun at Finn, who looked at it as if he had been handed a live snake, before burying it in a box of props.

Next Darrius took out his phone.

'So you didn't tell anyone? And to think I almost believed you. You, Ms Turnado, have just signed your friend's death warrant.'

'No, boss,' said Dmitri, almost choking on the words. 'They're not here for us.' He pointed at Kat. 'They're here for her.'

16

No one was more surprised than Kat. Everyone was looking at her but they turned as one when the flap of the tent was thrust aside and two men entered.

One was a uniformed police officer Kat didn't recognise. The other was . . . Paul?

Silence reigned as Paul surveyed the crowd. His gaze lingered for an incredulous second on Noodle, still in full costume, before coming to rest on Kat.

He held up his ID for all to see.

'Detective Inspect Stafford.' There was no expression on his face whatsoever. 'You.' He pointed at Kat. 'I want a word with you.'

She was so shocked to see him that she couldn't speak. Not so Darrius.

'What is this about?' he demanded.

Paul's expression didn't change.

'And you are, sir?'

'Darrius Bell. I'm the ringmaster here and I demand to know what's going on.'

By not so much as a flicker did Paul give away that he knew the name.

'This doesn't concern you, sir.' Again he looked at Kat. 'Shall we?'

Jake jumped in. 'Is she under arrest?'

Paul narrowed his gaze on him. 'No.'

'Then you can't just barge in her and take her.'

'Which is why I'm asking nicely,' said Paul. 'But if she doesn't want to respond nicely, then we'll continue this conversation down at the station.'

He meant it, too. Her boss wasn't a tall man, or particularly muscular. But when he was in the mood he had a physical presence and authority that few could stand up to. And he was most definitely in that mood right now. In fact she could tell he was furious.

'This is outrageous,' blustered Darrius.

'It's OK.' Kat finally found her voice. 'I'll speak to him.'

'Very wise,' said Paul. 'Now is there

somewhere more private?'

'You can speak to her here,' said Darrius.

'Yes, I could,' snapped Paul, losing his patience. 'But here's the thing. I don't want to. If you or anyone else has a problem with that, you can explain your objections down at the station. Do I make myself clear?'

He was bluffing, Kat knew. He had no grounds to question her or anyone here. But he was utterly intimidating.

Jake, however, wasn't cowed.

'If she's not under arrest she doesn't have to go anywhere with you. Kat, say nothing until we get you a lawyer.'

Noodle, Marty and the others were getting over their shock. Kat could see them growing indignant.

'It's OK,' she said quickly. 'Jake, can we use your caravan?'

'I'm coming with you,' he said.

'As am I,' said Darrius smartly.

Paul shook his head.

'I don't think any of you are quite getting this, so let me be clear. She's the one I want. Neither of you two are going anywhere.'

Jake shouldered past Kat.

'No, you're the one not getting it. You're not taking her.'

The atmosphere suddenly began to fizz. Xerxes cracked his knuckles. The uniformed constable's hand inched nervously towards his radio.

Paul, seemingly oblivious to the tension, stepped up to meet Jake, who was six inches taller.

'You don't want to do this, lad.'

'Try me.'

Paul glanced past him to Kat, and she nodded almost imperceptibly.

'Fine, you can come.'

'What about me?' demanded Darrius.

'Don't push it,' snapped Paul. 'Gallagher,' he told the constable, 'everyone stays here until I'm done.'

Outside, the evening was dark and cool.

'Which way?' asked Paul.

She pointed wordlessly and he marched them there in silence. Inside

Jake's caravan, he closed the door and stood with his back to it, arms folded.

'Sit down, both of you,' he commanded.

She sat. Jake didn't. Instead he squared his feet and folded his arms, mimicking Paul's stance.

Paul sighed. 'There's always one, isn't there?'

'Paul, I can explain.'

'Oh, I certainly hope so.'

'You know this guy?' asked Jake in shock.

Paul ignored him.

'What have you got yourself into this time, kid?' he asked Kat.

Jake was looking from one to the other in utter confusion.

'It's OK, Jake,' Kat told him. 'Paul, I can't tell you. I'm sorry, but I'm asking you to trust me.'

'Trust works both ways, Lyn.'

'I know. I admit there is something going on here. I'm trying to sort it. Can you give me time?'

'Has a crime been committed?'

asked Paul.

Kat couldn't lie to her friend and mentor. She chewed her lip wondering what to do.

Luckily Jake had had enough.

'Who the hell are you?' he asked Paul. 'And who the hell is Lyn? Kat, what is going on?'

'Who is Kat?' countered Paul.

'I'm Kat. My full name is Katelyn, remember,' she told Paul before turning to Jake. 'I changed my name when I left here. I use Lyn on the outside.'

'She does. And just to clear up any confusion,' said Paul, 'I'm here to speak to Lyn Turner. My DS. She's in a bit of bother, you see. But that's not unusual, is it, Lyn?'

Kat hung her head. This was a nightmare. She didn't dare look at Jake.

'DS?' he asked.

'Detective Sergeant,' said Paul helpfully.

'You're a police officer?' Jake asked, incredulous.

She nodded, face aflame.

'Are you investigating us?' Jake demanded.

'No! I honestly came to see Delilah.'

'And you claimed we were keeping secrets.'

'Jake, please. I was going to tell you. But can this keep till later?'

Paul observed this exchange with interest.

'Ah — so this is the guy who broke your heart all those years ago and made you fall into the arms of that con man.'

'What?' asked Jake, and Kat had the impression he was about to explode.

'Calm yourself, lad,' said Paul affably. 'She has that effect on lots of people. So, Lyn, what's going on? When you didn't get back to me I got worried. Can you assure me you're OK?'

'You called me?' She checked her phone. Half a dozen missed calls, all while she was asleep this afternoon. 'I am. OK, I mean.'

'Are you sure?'

'I'm sure, Paul. These people are my friends.'

'All of them?'

'Well, no,' she admitted. 'We've had some trouble but we're handling it.'

'That's right,' said Jake belligerently. 'We're handling it. So if you don't have any more questions . . .'

The two men glared at each other, no love lost.

'Are you going to guarantee her safety?' asked Paul.

'Absolutely.'

Paul held his eye a moment longer then nodded.

'Well, OK. I'll hold you to that. And you, Lyn, there are limits. If I find out you are messing where you shouldn't be, it'll be me you answer to, not anyone else. Understood?'

'Yes.'

'Yes what?'

'Yes, sir.'

'Good. Now the reason I called. Dominic Brixton? AKA Darrius Bell. The pompous one in the tent?'

'Yes. Did you find anything?' she asked eagerly.

'A sealed juvie record. A series of charges in his early twenties that never stuck. One court case that collapsed when the only witness changed their statement. Since then, nada. Slippery as a wet eel, that one, and my guess — as bad as they come.'

She and Jake looked at each other.

'What was he charged with?' asked Kat.

'Aggravated assault. Armed robbery. Not a nice guy. OK.' Paul rolled his shoulders. 'Now, since lover boy here clearly didn't know about your job, I take it it's a big secret. So why don't I march you back to your friends and continue my bad cop routine?'

As they walked back, Jake caught her arm.

'A police officer, Kat?'

'It's complicated,' she said. 'I promise I'll explain everything.'

'Come along boys and girls,' called Paul. He waited until they caught up. 'They'll want to know what this was about. Better have a story ready.'

'Um, yeah. Parking ticket?' she suggested.

'I came down a bit hard for that,' said Paul.

He was right. On both counts. Kat knew there would be a reception waiting for them. It wasn't just Darrius who would be full of questions.

An idea was reluctantly forming in her mind. Everything in her rebelled against it but she couldn't see a better way to allay Darrius' suspicions. In fact, it might be the only way to make him trust her.

'I can say it was about Nathan's investigation.'

Paul's eyes filled with sympathy. He knew she had come here to get away from all that.

'Good luck, kid. Keep in touch.'

There was a warning in that last sentence.

'I will. Bye,' she said softly.

'I would ask who Nathan is but I'm beginning to sound like an echo,' grumbled Jake.

'I know and I'm sorry.'

Paul continued on past the entrance to the circus tent, calling to his constable.

'Gallagher. Let's go.'

Without a backward glance at Kat, or see if Gallagher was following, he kept walking.

'Jake,' she said urgently. 'I'm going to do something that may not make sense to you but —'

Darrius stuck his head out of the tent, interrupting. 'Ms Turnado. Jacob. We're waiting, if you please?'

Too late. She sagged wearily. The day wasn't over yet. Not by a long shot.

* * *

Kat's friends greeted her with concern.

'Are you all right?'

'What did he want? He was a right bully.'

'I'm fine,' she assured them, both touched by their concern and ashamed of what she was going to do next.

Darrius cleared his throat. He had the

gun in his hand once more and saw Kat looking.

'Luckily our resident clown here kept PC Plod entertained with a few magic tricks, which prevented him from nosing around, or things could have got messy. Now you two, I feel a story coming on and it had better be a good one. What, pray tell, did the police want?'

The day armed officers had burst into Kat's home at dawn and arrested Nathan had felt like the worst of her life. She'd had to stand in her pyjamas watching her colleagues search her house. Not one would look at her. The shame had been overwhelming.

What she was about to do was worse.

Kat took a breath, and tossed her head.

'Do an online search on me,' she told Darrius.

'Why would I do that?'

'It's easier and quicker than me explaining. Not Kat Turnado. Lyn Turner. I was christened Katelyn Turner but use Lyn for my own reasons.'

Darrius was suspicious but he nodded

to Finn, who did as he was told. Some of the others were already doing the same. Finn's eyebrows shot up and he handed the phone to Darrius who read the screen, a slow smile spreading over his face.

Instead of smiles, Noodle, Xerxes and Marty were frowning.

Jake's eyes were darting everywhere and she recognised that once familiar panic she'd last seen at school when he wasn't able to follow the lesson. Of course he wouldn't be able to search his phone like the others, or at least not quickly or under this type of pressure. Her heart ached that she was the cause of his frustration and she was relieved when Noodle took his arm and began to whisper to him.

'Detective Sergeant Lyn Turner,' said Darrius. 'You have been a naughty girl. And your boyfriend is even worse by all accounts. Not much of a judge of character, are you?'

'Or maybe I'm an excellent judge of character,' she suggested with a defiance she didn't feel.

Darius smiled like a shark.

'Maybe you are, at that. A bent cop.' He laughed so hard he almost choked. 'This is incredible. I could never have planned for this. Nor could I have asked for a more convincing accomplice.'

Kat could feel the confusion emanating from her friends. The expression on poor Nellie's face would haunt her forever. She didn't dare look at Jake.

She wanted to fall through the floor and simply disappear. Instead she raised her chin and smiled.

'So, to get back to the conversation before we were rudely interrupted, how do we steal a Tintoretto? More to the point, what's our cut?'

17

The group dispersed soon after that. Darrius to plan how he could use this new information; the others because, as Jake reminded them, they still had to work tomorrow.

He could see that Kat was practically dead on her feet. He knew how she felt; this morning's walk with little Maddie seemed like a lifetime ago.

'We'll talk about it tomorrow,' he told everyone.

'But Jake,' whispered Marty. 'Did Kat really do those things? I mean, she can't be serious about stealing the painting — can she?'

Those were very much Jake's thoughts too.

'Tomorrow,' he repeated firmly.

Jake had never felt as useless as he had when everyone was reading up about Kat on their phones. He'd stood there like an idiot until Noodle had told him what was going on.

Even now he couldn't believe it. Organised crime? Money laundering? The Kat he knew would never have been involved in anything like that.

But then, the Kat he knew had been gone a long time. And hadn't he always suspected that she had come here, running from something?

But no. Jake might struggle with the written word, but he was excellent at reading people and Kat was as straight as they came. That guy Paul, her boss, had been concerned about her, too. He would have behaved very differently if he thought she was dodgy in any way.

'We don't know anything for sure,' he told Marty. 'And everyone's tired.' He raised his voice. 'Go home, get some sleep,' he told everyone. 'We'll talk tomorrow.'

Slowly they drifted away, looking troubled.

Kat had plonked down on a box as if her legs would no longer hold her up.

'They hate me,' she said when they

were alone.

'They're confused,' said Jake. 'Lots to take in.'

She raised her tear-stained face.

'I should have told you earlier, shouldn't I? About Nathan. About my job.'

'We should probably both have been more honest with each other,' he conceded. 'Come on. Let's get you back.'

She was too weary to protest, allowing him to pull her to her feet and walk her slowly back to the caravan.

'Will you be all right?' he asked at her bedroom door. 'Do you want me to get you anything to eat?'

'I just need sleep,' she said, then added, 'I'm sorry about this afternoon. For doubting you. Thank you for telling me.'

That seemed a lifetime ago.

'I'm sorry too. Goodnight.'

'Jake?' she stopped him once more. 'I didn't do it. I didn't do any of those things you read about.'

'I know,' he said, and in that moment

he did. This was Kat; the woman he had loved for most of his life. 'Everything will seem better in the morning.'

He hoped for all their sakes that it was true.

* * *

Kat stripped off and crept into bed, curling into a foetal position. How many worst days could one life have?

She couldn't sleep. One horrific scene after another from the day played in her head.

Learning the truth about her parents.

Darrius pointing a gun at her friends.

Paul, so cold and formal.

The way Nellie had looked at her.

And Jake. How many shocks had she piled on him tonight? And yet he'd defended her, from Darrius, from Paul, and even from their friends.

She tossed and turned until finally she accepted that sleep wouldn't come. Quietly she rose from her bed, pulled on a pair of yoga pants and a cotton vest.

Padding out of the room, she tapped softly on his door. If he was asleep she'd just go back —

'Kat?' he said immediately. 'Is everything OK?'

She pushed the door open.

'Can I come in? I don't want to be alone.'

In answer he drew the covers back and she slipped in next to his warm body.

He wrapped her in his arms and she felt herself almost melt in relief.

'It's been a tough few weeks,' she admitted.

'I'm beginning to get that.'

They lay in silence and eventually her panic stilled. She could feel his heart beat against her back, strong and steady and maybe a little fast.

It felt good to be held. She'd been keeping people at an arm's length for so long now.

His breathing told her he was still awake.

'I met Nathan three years ago,' she said into the silence.

'You don't have to tell me anything.'

'I want to.'

She took a moment to order her thoughts. There had been so many hours of questioning after Nathan's arrest. She'd tried so hard to be clear and factual and answer everything to the best of her ability. But they'd made her repeat things over and over, trying to catch her out.

What all those hours of questioning hadn't dealt with were the emotions the questions brought up. Forced to relive her life with Nathan over and over, she'd seen their relationship in a whole new light. At the time the fun, the travel, the glamorous parties had seemed like a fairy tale. Through the eyes of her superiors, they turned naïve and seedy.

'His gallery was robbed. I was a brand-new detective constable and sent with my then sergeant to investigate.'

Nathan had been so good-looking, so charming. He'd taken an instant shine to her. Little had been taken in the robbery, so he was only reporting the theft for insurance purposes. Now she wondered if even that had been a scam.

'He asked me out straight away but of course I said no. He was persistent though, turning up with flowers and extravagant gifts. Even so, it was six months before I finally accepted.'

Life with Nathan had been a whirlwind.

'Eventually we got engaged and moved in together. Everything was great. His gallery was doing well. He had so much money he wanted to pay for everything, clothes, holidays, entertaining. I wasn't comfortable with that and insisted I pay my own way, using the money from the sale of my flat.

'And thank heavens I did. After his arrest they scrutinised absolutely everything to do with our finances, trying to prove I had benefited from the proceeds of his crimes.'

It had been touch and go — maybe still was — but she had bank statements and receipts to prove that what she was saying was true. The only thing Nathan had paid for was upgrades on their holidays. No way could she have afforded regular first-class travel and penthouse apartments on a police officer's salary, while he had refused to settle for anything less.

'I didn't go on as many holidays as he wanted because of my job, but he never applied any pressure. He knew how important it was to me.'

She grew silent. When she started speaking again, she heard her voice tremble.

'We'd had a weekend away at the wedding of one of Nathan's oldest friends in New York and arrived back late on Sunday night. The gallery was closed the next day but I had to get up for work so we had an early night. Early in the morning there was a hammering at the door. We were both groggy and jet lagged, with no idea what was going on until suddenly there was an almighty crash. They b . . . broke the door down.'

Now she was shaking all over and was glad of Jake's arms around her.

'It was terrifying. Because of the serious nature of the allegations, a SWAT team stormed up the stairs. The bedroom was full of people in riot gear with lights on their helmets. Everybody was yelling. I wasn't even allowed to get dressed before being handcuffed and taken downstairs. Thankfully someone gave me a robe.'

That someone was a woman Kat had gone through training with. They'd been for a drink the week before. Now she wouldn't even look at Kat.

'And Nathan?'

'Nathan was yelling and demanding his lawyer and to see their warrant. I mean, I was the police officer but he was the one who was ready for this. I think he'd always been ready.

'He saw me as they led him down the stairs. He told me not to say anything.'

That had pretty much damned her in the eyes of her colleagues.

'They took all his papers, his electronics. Mine too. A senior officer arrived and formally told me that I was suspended, that I was to have no contact with Nathan or any of his associates and that I should present myself at the station the next day for formal questioning.'

'What was he charged with?'

'Benefiting from the proceeds of crime. And more specifically, 'criminal property acquisition and removing said property from the country.' Would you believe that includes art theft?'

'Ouch,' said Jake.

'I was questioned, shamed and shunned. The press had a field day — the detective who couldn't detect major crime going on under her nose. They were camped outside the house every day.'

She considered carefully what to say next. This was something she hadn't even told Paul.

'And then . . . one day I had a visit. I have no idea who he was. By this time I was used to dodging the press and I came home via the back gardens only to find a strange man in my kitchen. He told me to keep my mouth shut.'

'But you weren't part of this!' Jake was outraged.

'I know, but it was a warning. Luckily I'd already been speaking to Delilah and as soon as she heard what was going on, she invited me here.'

'And walked into this. Sorry,' murmured Jake.

'Not your fault. I'm afraid Darrius wasn't wrong about my lack of judgment.'

He stroked her hair. 'We'll sort this, Kat.'

His faith was gratifying. Should she tell him the rest? The secret that kept her awake at night? The thing that could still end her career?

She simply didn't have the reserves left.

'Get some sleep,' he said. 'I'll be here when you wake up.'

* * *

Jake was up before her the next day. Everything she had told him had been disturbing but it didn't change how he felt about her.

With Kat's permission, he told the others everything in quick, hushed conversations.

'I knew there had to be an explanation,' said Nellie, loyally. 'I knew our Kat wasn't like that.'

'Maybe she can give us some tips on nicking the painting,' grinned Marty. 'Joke,' he added quickly as Jake glowered at him. 'I'm sorry for what she's been through — poor kid leaves here to start a new life and gets dumped on. The police aren't very loyal if they treat their own like that, are they?'

'That guy last night was actually a friend,' said Jake grudgingly.

'You what? Got a funny way of showing it.'

'He was worried about her. But just so you know, she hasn't told him any of this. She says he'll have to report it if he knows.'

'Understood,' said Marty. 'So what next?'

'We hope to get a lead from Dmitri or Finn.'

'Time's getting on, Jake. We're only here another four days. Something has to give before then.'

'I know. We're meeting Darrius later to find out his plans, even if we have none of our own.'

18

Jake had been adamant he would be accompanying Kat when Darrius sent for her, but she'd put her foot down.

'You've already shown him the sort of man you are. He won't buy any sudden change in your character. Whereas if he thinks I'm dodgy, he might slip up and give something away. We have so little to go on, we need to use every advantage we have.'

'I just don't like the idea of you being alone with him. Or worse, with those two goons.'

'I think Finn's already gone off somewhere. Marty's following him — fingers crossed. I'll be fine.' She smiled. 'Helloo? Police officer here. I've been in worse situations.'

'I don't like to think about that either.'

'Says the daring young man on the flying trapeze.' She kissed him lightly on the lips. 'You can wait here and come running if I scream.'

'That's not funny.' But he too, managed a smile.

Kat wasn't feeling so cocky as she knocked at the door of Darrius' caravan.

'Come in. It's not locked. Though that hasn't ever stopped you before, has it? Cup of tea?'

Unbelievably he had set out a tray of refreshments, as if this was a social visit.

'No thanks.'

'To business, then. No doubt the Scooby gang have filled you in on everything?'

'Kidnapping, theft, coercion? Is that about right?'

He frowned. 'Just as a precaution, would you mind removing your clothes? I have to know you aren't wearing a wire.'

She rolled her eyes. 'I would mind that very much. But just to get this thing rolling . . .' She grabbed the bottom of her T-shirt and yanked it up, giving a twirl and flashing her lacy bra. Obviously her shorts were not hiding much. 'Satisfied?'

Over by the door Dmitri made a choking sound but Darrius didn't react.

'Thank you. Would you like me to reciprocate?'

'Please don't.'

Darrius poured himself some tea before getting right down to business.

'There are two things I need from you. First, you must worm your way back into Huntersly's library and return with a plan on how to execute this robbery.'

'How am I supposed to do that?'

'A blend of circus talent and whatever sleuthing skills you picked up on the job. I'd imagine the villains who were caught are not the ones to copy, but what do I know? Be aware the clock is ticking. This is Wednesday. I believe we up sticks on Saturday. This has to be done by then.'

The idea of seeking out Lord Huntersly, then pumping him for information, made her feel sick.

'Since you're our very own villain, why don't you have a plan?'

'I do and I'm executing it beautifully,' said Darrius. 'First I find something worth stealing, then I intimidate people into doing my bidding while I sit back and reap the results.'

He looked infinitely pleased with himself.

'You do know it will be almost impossible to pull this off without getting caught?' Kat told him.

'Not my problem. In fact, my only real role in this is to collect the painting and my money,' he said smugly.

'And release Delilah unhurt,' she reminded him sharply.

'Yes. That too.'

'So you won't actually be participating in the robbery?' She stored that information away.

'Certainly not. I aim to have a cast-iron alibi.'

Kat had had enough of Darrius' company and Dmitri's leering.

'And the second thing? You said there are two.'

'Oh, yes — that one's much easier. All I want is an introduction to your gallery owner fiancé.'

She hadn't seen that coming.

'You have got to be kidding,' she said in shock.

'I'm afraid not. Although I've had some modest success in my career, this theft raises me to a whole new tier of the hierarchy,' he said with relish. 'The people who have handled things for me in the past will simply not have the necessary connections to take on something of this magnitude.'

'And you think Nathan can help you?'

She tried to keep her voice neutral even as her mind raced. Nathan was the past. She wanted nothing to do with him. Besides, Paul had warned her specifically to stay well away from him.

'Then you're wrong. He's locked up,' she lied.

'Wrong,' said Darrius. 'He was released on bail two days ago.' His eyes danced. He was enjoying the game, showing how clever he was. Hopefully his over-confidence would be his downfall.

'I wouldn't presume to know the full

details of your relationship with Nathan Barnes but I know you have met his contacts. So many photos of you with so many shady people.' He shook his head.

She hadn't known they were shady! To her they had just been Nathan's rich friends. She hadn't exactly been attending illegal auctions of stolen art. As far as she was concerned they had been gala dinners, christenings, birthday parties. How was she supposed to know every crime family in the world, especially the foreign ones?

Besides, these people were notorious for guarding their privacy. Kat was usually the only numpty in the group facing the camera!

Ignorance was a weak defence; she'd seen that in her interrogators' eyes. But it was the truth.

'Nathan won't see me,' she lied. Actually he'd tried to contact her many times before she'd run off to the circus, but she'd refused to take his calls.

'That's OK,' said Darrius. 'I took the liberty of contacting him for you.'

'You did what?' She shot forward in her seat.

'Relax. It was just a text. I used a burner phone, of course, and pretended to be you. I didn't tell him where you were. Just that you wanted to meet.'

No. No. No. On top of everything that was going on, how could she be expected to deal with Nathan, too?

'How did you get his details?'

Another shark smile.

'I'm a criminal, Ms Turnado. One can find anything if one is has the right connections and is prepared to pay.'

'And he agreed?'

She hadn't spoken to Nathan since that day he was marched out of the house, wearing nothing but a pair of pyjama bottoms so low-slung they were only held on by a prayer. What a great picture that had made. Blond, tanned, six-pack, smiling for the cameras and cheerfully protesting his innocence. He'd been on the front page of every newspaper.

Nerves tangled like snakes in her stomach. Why on earth would he want to speak to her? To issue another warning? Or because he wanted something from her? This was a complication she could do without.

'He's very keen to meet,' said Darrius. He tossed a phone into her lap. 'The details are on there. I know it may harm your case if you are caught contacting him but, well, that's not my problem.'

'And what do you want from this meeting?'

'That's easy. I want to know how to smuggle the painting abroad. And I want an invitation to the next dark auction.'

Dark auction. Where absolutely anything could be bought or sold for the right price.

Darrius, looking supremely satisfied with himself, munched on a shortbread finger.

'Unless you want to flash poor Dmitri again, I think that concludes our business for today. You are going to be quite busy, aren't you?' He dismissed her with a contemptuous finger wave. 'Hop, hop,

Ms Turnado. And never forget — your friend is relying on you.'

* * *

Jake was pacing. She told him about Lord Huntersly but not about the meeting with Nathan.

'I'll come with you,' he said immediately.

'No. It's easier for me to casually bump into him on my own.'

And if everything went belly-up, she would take the fall all by herself.

It was criminal just how easy it was to waylay Lord Huntersly. Kat had noticed that he walked down to the paddock with treats for the horses every afternoon, staying on the Huntersly side of the high metal fence. All she had to do was be in the paddock, grooming Phaedra's gleaming herd, when he arrived.

'Kat. How lovely to see you.'

'And you, Lord H. Taking a constitutional? Do you want some company?' How she hated herself.

'Always, my dear.'

She climbed over the fence easily.

'Not that I can walk far these days. Just a turn around the garden usually, but I like to get out.'

Kat fell in beside him, matching her stride to his much slower one. When she was little she'd jumped and skipped along the paths and clambered over stone lions in the formal gardens while her parents and Lord Huntersly chatted about boring things.

'Is the show going well?' he asked.

'Sold out,' she said. 'We love coming here.'

'I'm truly sorry about all the extra security.'

Why did he have to be so nice?

'That's not your fault. Anyway, you can't be too careful these days. No one minds.'

Their path took them behind the Hall, just as Kat planned.

'We don't keep horses now, what with my health failing,' said Lord Huntersly as they passed the old stable block. 'The boys don't think it's worthwhile to have them around eating their heads off.'

The boys could take a running jump as far as Kat was concerned.

'You can come and see ours any time. They love attention.'

'Thank you, my dear. Marcus wants to turn the stable block into a tearoom and have paying visitors in the house. I'm afraid I've outlived my time here.'

He sounded forlorn.

Kat railed inwardly at Marcus. Couldn't he wait until he actually inherited to make changes?

'Did I ever tell you how your mother and I met?'

Lord Huntersly was off again, retelling the much-loved tale. Kat could answer and nod in all the right places, so she turned her attention to the house.

The gothic architecture was still in evidence at the back but much toned down. Fewer gargoyles and not so many carved mouldings on the arched windows. With the house built on a slope, the ground floor windows here were lower than at the front and mainly served the kitchens and store rooms. Most of them were barred, though Lord Huntersly had steadfastly refused to do the same at the front.

'A prisoner in my own home? Not while I draw breath,' he declared.

From this aspect, all the grand public rooms in the house appeared to be on the first floor. This meant that the ballroom, in the centre of the house, was graced with tall, floor-to-ceiling windows and a grand balcony with sweeping stone steps leading down to the garden.

Kat dismissed the ground and first floor windows. One floor was barred, the second almost definitely alarmed. The second floor windows were new and probably alarmed too.

But the windows on the third floor were far more interesting. Sash windows, older and unbarred. And who would alarm a third floor window with a forty-foot drop? They looked like a good way in.

So how to get up there?

There were several drainpipes on the walls. Not a burglar's friend in these modern times of plastic, but with a listed building like this, Kat knew they would be good old-fashioned cast iron. Easy enough for almost anyone with circus training to scale, especially with balconettes on many of the windows for added footholds.

She mentally chose the easiest drainpipe for her needs, then counted the windows so she could place it from inside the house.

Lord Huntersly saw her looking at the building but mistook her interest.

'You're admiring the Virginia creeper, aren't you? It's practically a weed, of course, but so pretty in the autumn. Marcus wants to get rid of that too.'

'It is pretty,' Kat agreed, thinking she might want to kill Marcus. She realised his Lordship was out of puff. 'Are you tired? Do you want to go back?'

'Perhaps I should,' he said. 'You will come in for tea? Cook has made those cakes you like.'

'I'd love to,' said Kat, hating herself more and more by the minute.

19

They wound their way slowly back to the front of the house after Lord Huntersly helpfully offered the information that all the doors at the back were locked and alarmed, so best not to use them.

Jamieson opened the door as if he lived behind it.

'Thank you, Jamieson. A pot of tea for two, please,' Lord Huntersly said as the butler helped him off with his coat. 'Shall we take it in the morning room, Kat?'

Her heart sank. How could she suggest she'd prefer the library without it looking too obvious? Lord Huntersly might be far too trusting; Jamieson was not.

His lordship followed her gaze.

'No, of course. It has to be the library. What am I thinking!'

'My lord,' said Jamieson. 'The security . . .'

'Away with them,' said Lord Huntersly crossly. 'I'll take tea where I like in my own house.'

'As you wish, my lord.' Jamieson melted away.

They were in the large, marbled foyer. Various doors and panelled passageways led off. Kat looked around surreptitiously. One wide-angle security camera in a corner on the ceiling, taking in the main entrance and the double staircase. A red light suggested it was probably recording them right now. There were no red lights glowing from any of the passageways — presumably the security firm was confident this one was all-encompassing.

Lord Huntersly went straight to a large Chinese vase on a spindly-legged table in a corner. Both table and vase were probably priceless but he tipped the vase slightly and dug his hand in.

'Should you be doing that?' worried Kat, thinking he was about to send one or both flying.

'Shhh,' His lordship produced a plastic keycard from inside the vase.

Kat glanced involuntarily up at the camera and he winked.

'The vase is in a blind spot. They wanted to put cameras all around, but this is still my house.'

One of the passageways came out just beneath the blind spot. Kat made a mental note.

'They put this new lock on the library after the painting was valued,' explained Lord Huntersly. 'They tried all sorts for an old codger like me. Keypad, eye recognition. Balderdash, all of it. I could never remember the damned number and did not approve of that thing beaming in my eyes. This is still my house, you know. They had to send someone every time I set it off. The boys were very cross.'

The twinkle in his eyes suggested he wasn't too upset by that.

'They'd have a fit if they knew I kept the key there, of course. But I'm far too old to be running around looking for it every time I need it, especially as I'm not even supposed to tell Jamieson where it is. Utter nonsense, the whole thing. The painting has been here for centuries. Why would someone steal it now, eh?'

Kat felt yet another rush of guilt as he opened the library door and showed her in.

'It's OK,' he said when she hesitated. 'The lasers only work at night.' He rolled his eyes. 'Listen to me. Laser beams. Like James Bond. Can you imagine? Plus there's the pressure thingy in front of the painting, of course. That's on all the time so you can't get close.'

Kat's cheeks were burning. Here he was giving her all the information she needed to rob him and he was doing it because he trusted her.

And she was about to make it worse.

'Can I use your loo?'

'Of course, my dear. There's a cloak-room just past the drawing room.'

'I remember.'

She found the cloakroom but hurried on past it to a door hidden in the wooden panelling at the end of the corridor. Not a secret passage, but servant's stairs she had found exploring as a child.

These days the Hall had only a fraction of the staff they'd once employed and the door was stiff, but with a good hard shove, she was in.

Then she took the stairs two at a time to the top floor. Three rooms along, she counted. Taking a deep breath she opened the door. No alarm and she let out a sigh of relief. It was a small bedroom — belonging to a governess or favoured servant perhaps, but clearly unused for half a century.

She ran to the window and looked out at the circus in the field below.

Another deep breath and she opened the window. Phew. No alarm here either. She stuck her head out — and yes! The drain pipe was easily reachable.

She pulled the window down, leaving it open an inch or two. Then she was back down the stairs quick as a flash and pulling the panelled door closed behind her.

She was hurrying to the library when she saw a figure blocking her way.

* * *

'Going somewhere?'

Marcus. Just what she needed.

'Just looking for the loo.'

'It's back there.'

'Oops. Silly me.'

He glanced over her shoulder.

'Yes, very silly. Or maybe you were up to something else, like a bit of petty pilfering. I'd be within my rights to search you.'

'I'm your father's guest. I'm allowed to use the bathroom,' said Kat, her heart rate accelerating.

'What's allowed and what actually happens are often two different things.'

He grabbed Kat's wrist and she was so surprised she didn't pull away.

'Not so cheeky now, are you?' leered Marcus as he pulled her against him. 'I always fancied taking you down a peg or two. You've always been an uppity little thing.'

Kat wasn't scared of him, but she was a guest in this house. Besides, the last thing she wanted was to cause a scene. She was still figuring out what to do when a noise behind them startled them both.

'Ahem.' Jamieson stood at a polite distance. I'm here to escort Ms Turnado back to the library, sir.'

Marcus let her go. 'Next time,' he told Kat.

She edged past him and the waiting butler. Marcus had been raised in this house. Even if he didn't remember the servants' stairs, there was no way Jamieson didn't know about them. If it came to it — and God forbid they actually had to steal the painting to save Delilah — both Jamieson and Marcus would remember this moment.

In the library Lord Huntersly was sitting by the fire. The tea tray was there, which explained why Jamieson had come looking for her, but his lordship appeared to have dozed off.

She didn't wake him but quickly checked out the room, knowing she would never have spotted the boxes that controlled the lasers if she hadn't been warned about them. Although she had half an idea how to deflect them, she suspected it would take a prayer and a healthy dose of luck. The pressure pad, she was pretty sure she could deal with.

Lord Huntersly stirred as she poured the tea.

'Sorry. Did I doze off?'

'Only for a minute,' she said gently.

They chatted until she saw his head begin to nod once more.

'You look tired. I should go now.'

'No, no.' He forced his eyes open but it was clearly a losing battle.

'It's almost time for the matinée anyway.'

'Ah yes. Of course, my dear. Then thank you for the company.'

She kissed his cheek and turned to go.

'Wait.'

'Yes?' Kat froze, her nerves jangling alarmingly. Had she given herself away? Been caught on some camera she hadn't noticed?

'Your father,' said Lord Huntersly

quietly. 'I told you he used to join me for a nightcap sometimes.'

'You did.' Kat glanced longingly at the door.

'Sometimes . . . well, sometimes he drank more than was probably good for him. I've always wondered if I should have said something to him. Or to Mara. Was . . . do you think the accident could have been my fault?'

'No,' said Kat immediately, taking his hand in both of hers. 'Never ever think that. Whatever happened that night was absolutely not your fault.'

'Thank you,' he murmured sleepily. 'You're a good girl, Kat. A credit to your mother.'

Guilt sat over her like a cloud as she made her way out. The next time she left this house, would she have a priceless painting under her arm?

Or would she be in handcuffs, having broken an old man's heart?

* * *

Everyone was milling around when she got back, some at least pretending to work. Jake didn't even bother doing that. The moment he saw her, he hurried to meet her.

'How did it go? Are you OK? Why are you so flushed? Did something happen?'

'Nothing happened. Everything went fine.' She lowered her voice. 'What about here? Did Marty find anything when he followed Finn?'

Jake shook his head. 'No. He went to the chemist.'

She tamped down her disappointment.

'There's still time. OK, I need to get changed for the show. We'll talk later.'

Between shows they all gathered in their usual place inside the big top and she laid out her plan.

'As you know, I've been up at the Hall looking for ways for us to get in. I think it can be done, but I thought I'd run my plans past everyone so we can iron out any problems before we take it to Darius,' she said.

People nodded.

'OK, you all know the general stuff. There are no guards onsite but there are perimeter alarms on doors and lower windows. The library door has key card access and the library itself is protected by a high tech laser security system. The painting is further protected by a pressure pad that sets off an alarm if anyone stands on it. As far as I can see, the lasers are the biggest problem. On the day of the robbery, I plan to go back and disable them.'

'How?' asked Nellie.

Kat had done some research online. But as a young constable she had covered a theft in a jeweller's shop with a similar system.

'The thief used mirrors to deflect them,' she explained. 'Since the beam wasn't broken, the alarm wasn't triggered. I can hardly take mirrors off the wall without anyone noticing, but there are two large, shiny, pottery foo dogs in the library . . .'

'Two large whats?' asked Marty.

'Chinese guard dogs, except they look more like lions. If I go late afternoon I can hopefully manage to move them in front of the sensors, then, when the beams are switched on, they should be deflected.'

Kat had no idea if any of this was true, but since if things went according to plan, the robbery was never going to happen, all she needed to do was sound convincing.

'That seems very technical but I'll trust you,' said Marty. 'How do we get in?'

She explained about the drainpipe and the open window. 'There are decorative balconies and the odd gargoyle to help us on our way. I'm confident it can be done, and I know for a fact that the window has no alarm.'

'I remember cast iron pipes,' said Noodle fondly. 'A burglar's dream. Ouch,' he added as Nellie elbowed him.

Kat told them about the servants' stairs, then drew a diagram showing the angle of the security camera. 'If we stick close to this wall, we should be OK.'

'Wouldn't it be safer to just disable the camera?' asked Marty.

She shook her head.

'Any interference like that might trigger a security check. I'm hoping if we can get in and out with little interference. They might not even notice straight away that the painting is gone.

'Here,' she pointed to just below the camera on her diagram, 'you'll find the key to the library.'

There were gasps.

'All that security,' said Marty sorrowfully. 'Some people don't deserve to have money.'

'And they don't deserve to get robbed either!' snapped Kat. 'Sorry,' she added quickly. 'I don't like any of this, though I know it has to be done.'

'So if we come out here,' said Jake, pointing at the diagram, 'get the key, stick to the wall like glue, we should be out of camera range all the way to the library door. It's not alarmed because the key card is considered to be deterrent enough. Fingers crossed the lasers are off. What about the pressure pad?'

Kat grinned. 'Here's the bit I'm hoping is clever. The library door is sturdy, solid oak. The painting hangs directly behind the door, not properly on display, which is why it never drew much attention. With the door open, I reckon someone could sit on the top of the door and hang down backwards by their knees, like on a trapeze. Then all they have to do is get the painting off the wall. Their feet will never touch the ground.'

'Nice.' Everyone nodded approvingly.

'Not something they'll have planned for,' agreed Jake.

As she'd hoped, no one protested that any of this was impossible. Circus people were the best.

But then everyone had been primed to go along with whatever she said, no matter how ridiculous it sounded.

'Then we reverse our steps, with the painting, and we're done.'

They heard the sound of a slow hand clap and Darrius stepped out from behind the curtain.

'Well done, Ms Turnado. Bravo.'

20

'You were listening!' accused Kat. Actually she had been counting on it.

'Of course. And I have to admit it all sounds extremely exciting. I almost wish I would be there to see it. I will, however, be there to recover the painting, and then I will depart. Your share will be paid when the painting sells. Perhaps we can work together again in the future.'

Over my dead body, thought Kat.

'Which of you will be participating in this masterful caper?' asked Darrius.

'Me,' said Jake immediately. 'Alone.'

'No way!' Various people voiced their protests.

'If it all goes wrong, only one of us need go down for it,' said Jake, practically.

'I'm coming too,' Kat piped up. 'I know the layout, the servants' stairs, and the camera.'

'There is absolutely no way you are

doing this,' repeated Jake.

'Children, children.' Darrius held up his hand. 'I'll leave the minor details to you. Ms Turnado, you have appeared like a shining light in the darkness to rescue this mission. I thank you from the bottom of my heart, but now, alas, I must be off.'

'Not so fast,' said Jake. 'Aren't you forgetting something? Delilah.'

'Ah, yes. As soon as we have the painting, I will of course tell you where you can pick her up.'

'No way,' said Jake to Kat's dismay.

What was he doing? Why was he stirring things? The plan was to rescue Delilah long before it ever reached this stage.

'I expect to see her from the window of the Hall,' said Jake. 'If I don't, the painting stays put.'

Of course! Relief flooded through her. Darrius would be suspicious if they didn't add this step. Thank goodness one of them was thinking straight.

'Fine, whatever.' Darrius agreed so

readily that Kat knew he had no intention of keeping his word. 'When does all this take place?' he asked.

'On our last night here,' said Kat. It was still four days away. 'If the theft is discovered, the chaos of pull down might provide some cover.'

'Excellent idea, Ms Turnado. You are remembering what else we talked about?'

'Yes,' said Kat.

'What was he talking about?' asked Jake once Darrius was gone.

'He, er . . . doesn't want me talking to Paul,' she mumbled, letting her hair swing in front of her face. It was the truth, just not all of it.

She hated more dishonesty, but could not see any advantage in telling Jake she had agreed to meet Nathan. Knowing him, he would insist on coming along, which would only complicate things.

* * *

'Do you think he bought it?' asked Jake when Phaedra, peering through the tent flap, gave them the nod that Darrius was truly gone.

'I think he's so blinded by the money, and the thought of climbing the criminal ladder, that he can't see anything else. What does everyone think of my plan?' Kat asked curiously.

'Might work,' said Jake.

'So-so,' said Noodle.

'Is that it?' She was ridiculously disappointed.

Suddenly they were all laughing and talking at once and she realised they were teasing her.

'Great plan.' Noodle slapped her on the back. 'If I'm ever tempted to get back into burglary, I'll definitely call on you.'

'Ahem. You do remember you're talking to a police officer,' Kat reminded him.

* * *

The show had to go on, and Kat finally made her debut in Xerxes' knife throwing act that evening. The crowd loved it, especially when her fake ponytail was sliced right off.

After the show, she and Jake snuggled up in his caravan. She sank onto his bed and into his arms, and despite the very real feeling of danger surrounding them, she had never felt so protected.

'What do we do if we can't find her?' asked Jake, voicing her biggest fear. 'We haven't had much luck so far.'

'We go to the police,' said Kat immediately. 'They'll make him tell.'

'We could make him tell,' said Jake. 'Tie him to Xerxes' knife-throwing board and I'm pretty sure he will tell us anything we want to know.'

'Torture is against the law,' she said, giggling at that image.

'What about failure to report a kidnapping? Isn't that illegal too?'

'You have a point. Then there's possession of an unregistered firearm.'

'Breaking and entering?' suggested Jake.

'You're forgetting conspiring to commit a crime.' They were both laughing now.

‘That’s the problem with dating a police officer,’ murmured Jake. ‘There’s no hiding anything.’

‘We’re dating?’

He drew her closer. ‘Is that too old-fashioned?’

‘I think it sounds just perfect.’

‘I can’t wait to get Delilah back and for life to return to normal,’ he said, nuzzling her neck.

Kat wasn’t sure she knew what normal was any more. Though falling asleep in Jake’s arms every night was definitely on the right track.

* * *

‘Any plans for today?’ asked Jake over breakfast.

‘I have to go into town,’ Kat said vaguely. ‘Can I borrow a car?’

‘Of course.’

‘What about you? What are you up to?’

‘Phaedra thinks one of the horses is a bit lame. We’re waiting for the vet.’

She kissed his cheek. ‘See you later.’

Kat left, feeling only a tiny bit guilty. She had no idea how this meeting with Nathan would go, but she suspected that having Jake tag along would not make it go any more smoothly.

What to wear to meet the ex-fiancé who had turned out to be a criminal mastermind? Eventually she settled on black jeans, sandals and a sky-blue tank top. Nice and neutral. She combed her long hair and left it loose about her shoulders. Make-up was no more than mascara and a slick of lip-gloss.

When she reached the circus car park, a man in a parked car rolled down his window and beckoned her over.

'Kat, can you do me a favour?'

Her jaw dropped. 'Noodle?'

In amazement she took in his brown corduroy trousers, short-sleeved shirt and scrubbed face. He had male pattern baldness and a rather large nose, even without the red ping-pong ball.

'I'm on tailing duty and I have a good feeling. Both Dmitri and Finn are leaving the ground this morning — Nellie heard them talking at breakfast — and they're taking two cars. Marty and I are ready in case they go in different directions.'

Kat could have told him that one of them would be following her, but he'd find out soon enough.

'You don't think they'll recognise you?'

'Admit it; you barely recognised me,' he said, looking pleased with himself.

That was true. If they did spot him, they'd think they were being followed by a geography teacher.

'What's the favour?' she asked.

'Cover for me in the show if I'm not back?'

Her meeting definitely shouldn't take that long.

'No problem.'

A flash of red in the back seat caught her attention. 'Captain's going with you?'

'You know I can't leave him alone. Besides, he's great company on a stake-out.'

'Isn't he a bit obvious?'

'We've been practising. Watch. Captain, hide.'

The bird tucked his head under his wing.

'Properly,' ordered Noodle.

Muttering, Captain used his powerful beak and claws to manoeuvre himself to the floor.

'Are we there yet?' he muttered.

Kat was laughing as she left them to it.

* * *

She had arranged to meet Nathan in a café in town. He rose immediately to his feet when he saw her, pecking her cheek before she could draw away. Lord, he was handsome. Appreciative sighs from other women in the café sent paper napkins wafting from tables onto the floor.

'So good to see you, Lyn,' he said warmly, his extraordinarily white teeth gleaming against his glowing skin.

'A tan, Nathan?' He'd been on remand for weeks.

'Sunbed. Got to keep up appearances.

I have to say, you look fabulous. I can see my concern about you was misplaced.'

There was a question in his words she didn't answer. Hard physical work, combined with plenty of time outdoors, had brought colour to her cheeks.

He reached for her hand but Kat was quicker, clenching her fist as she pulled away. The waitress, who had just arrived to take her order, shot her a disapproving look for treating this God-like creature so shabbily.

She ordered coffee. Nathan sat back.

'Hmm. I'm detecting a rather cool air. I take it this isn't where we book into a nice hotel, order champagne and fall into bed for fabulous make-up-for-lost-time sex?'

'That's right. This isn't that.'

He didn't seem too bothered.

'Come on Kat, lighten up. We have lots to celebrate; after all we're both free. But, OK, I'll bite. If not for the sex, then why are we here?

Darrius had arranged this meeting to enlist Nathan's help selling the

Tintoretto. Since Kat had no intention of stealing the painting, let alone selling it, she didn't even bother to bring it up. She could see Finn, sitting at the bus stop across the road. Hopefully he had already called Darrius to say she had made contact, so in theory she could just walk out any time now.

'Someone came to my house and threatened me,' she said instead.

His expression told her this wasn't news.

'You sent him?' she asked, surprised by how much that upset her. She'd still harboured some little hope that he wasn't involved.

'Not to threaten you,' he said quickly. 'It should have been more of a friendly warning, considering that you hadn't been returning my calls.'

'And that's supposed to be OK?' The man had terrified her, invading her home. 'Warning about what?'

'To keep your mouth shut, of course.'

'You of all people know I don't know anything.'

'Please,' he said dismissively. 'Don't play the innocent.'

'I'm not playing anything!'

'Come on, Lyn, you knew what was going on. I mean, ask yourself, did you ever see a customer in my gallery?'

She frowned. 'I . . .'

'Where do you think my money came from?'

'I thought you were a businessman.'

'I am. You knew what was going on but you chose to ignore it. Don't be so holier than thou.'

This was outrageous. 'I did not!'

'No? What about the necklace?'

Heat flooded her cheeks. There was no point in pretending she didn't know what he was talking about. At that last weekend in New York, Nathan had presented her with a fabulous diamond and sapphire necklace that not only perfectly matched her dress, but brought out the colour of her eyes.

'You told me it wasn't real.'

'I lied. And you knew I was lying. Who doesn't know the difference between

Fabergé and something off a market stall?'

It was true. She'd suspected the necklace was real but had honestly thought he'd just splurged madly on a gift for her. Which was why, after the wedding, she'd asked him to take it back as it was too extravagant.

'It never showed up in evidence,' she said.

'No. I sold it that weekend. The necklace was the real reason for the trip to New York, by the way. It's probably tucked away in some millionaire's vault by now. The police have no way of linking it to me, and I have the only photos of my fiancé wearing it.'

'You leaked that photo to the papers!'

He grinned. 'I don't know what you're talking about.'

'The picture was blurry,' she said desperately. The police clearly hadn't made the connection yet.

'Luckily I have other pictures,' said Nathan.

'Why?' she asked, not understanding.

'They will incriminate you too.'

'Exactly,' said Nathan. 'So releasing any more pictures would only ever be a last resort. I'm glad you understand. We can simply call them my insurance against you suddenly remembering anything that might be inconvenient. No hard feelings, eh?'

He was like a completely different man. How could she ever have thought she loved him?

'Was any of it real?' she blurted.

'All of it,' he said immediately, this time successfully capturing her hand in his. 'Every last minute. I adored you. We could have had a fantastic life together. Still can . . . ?'

'From prison?'

'That isn't part of the plan,' he said confidently. 'What do you say?'

A shadow passed over their table.

'Am I interrupting anything?' asked Jake.

21

Kat looked up at him with wide-eyed shock, but Jake was focused on her companion. Did women seriously go for over-baked tans and gym muscles? This guy had fake written all over him.

'What are you doing here?' said Kat.

'I could ask you the same thing.'

'Does Darrius know you are here?'

She slid her hand out from under the other man's and tucked it under the table.

'Who is Darrius?' The man spoke.

'I wasn't speaking to you,' snapped Jake.

'This is Nathan,' said Kat, resignedly. 'Nathan, Jake.'

'Jake? The man you ran away from? The one who broke your heart?' asked Nathan. He looked Jake up and down. 'Handsome. A bit of a diamond in the rough.'

'That's me,' said Jake. 'Which presumably makes you the money-laundering ex.'

'Please, call me Nathan. Lyn here calls me darling.' He winked at Kat and Jake saw her jaw tighten. Nathan stood up.

'Well, as always, lovely seeing you, Lyn. Perhaps one day after this is over we can have that drink. I'll be off. Remember, I have something of yours.'

He strolled out, stopping to flirt briefly with the waitress on the way.

Jake sat in the seat he'd vacated.

'What did he mean by that? And why did it sound like a threat?'

Kat shook her head wearily.

'What are you doing here?'

'Marty phoned to say he was following Finn, who appeared to be following you. I came immediately and swapped places with him. So, this is the job Darrius was talking about?'

She nodded. 'I'm supposed to get information from Nathan about how to sell the painting on.'

'Did you?'

'Of course not. We're not stealing it, remember?'

'So why did you come?'

Not by a flicker did he reveal the fear with which he awaited her answer. Once more he'd begun to fantasise that when this was all over, he and Kat might be able to have some kind of future together. But for all he knew, she was still hankering after a different kind of life with a different kind of man.

'Can we go for a walk?' she asked.

'Sure.' They rose to their feet, which was when Jake discovered Nathan had left them with the bill. He paid the waitress, who was enjoying the drama.

Kat was waiting for him in the street. Back was the pale face, the drawn look which he hated.

'Don't look now, but Finn is over there at the bus stop,' she informed him.

'I know. Give me two minutes.'

That was as long it took for Jake convince Finn to move on.

'Let's walk by the canal,' she said and led him down a path. They sat on a sunny bench.

'I told you what Nathan's been charged with,' she began.

He nodded.

'And that my defence is that I had no idea what he was up to and didn't benefit from his crimes.'

Another nod. Jake completely believed that.

'Well, there's a photo of me at a wedding wearing a very expensive stolen necklace. I didn't know it was stolen but Nathan is threatening to bring it to the attention of the police as proof that I'm not as innocent as I claim.'

She touched her throat as if remembering the weight of the necklace.

'Anyway, I wore it and it caused quite a stir at the wedding. Little did I know I was actually modelling it for the sale,' she said bitterly. 'Nathan had assured me it was fake, but I didn't quite believe him. It actually made me pay more attention to the other wedding guests, and I realised that Nathan's friends weren't just rich, they were mega-rich. For the first time I began to wonder how he could afford to be mixing in these circles.

'I didn't know what to do. I was going to talk my suspicions over with Paul when we got back, only I never got the chance before the raid.'

Jake digested this. Wearing the necklace, mixing with these people was probably not enough to convict her of anything, but it would certainly sow the seeds of doubt in her colleagues. It would be hard for her to return to policing if the pictures came out.

'Who saw you wearing it?'

'Everyone at the wedding. One of them must have sent the photos to Nathan.'

'What does he plan to do with the information?'

'Nothing. He says it's just insurance in case I say anything.'

But she would have this hanging over her head for evermore. He squeezed her hand.

'It's not the end of the world.'

'No. Just potentially the end of my career.' She rested her head on his shoulder. 'Do you know what? I feel better.'

He braced himself. 'For seeing Nathan?'

'No, silly. For telling you. Finally no more secrets between us.'

Jake's smile froze. Suddenly he just wanted to take his life and shake it hard, like a duvet on an unmade bed, in an effort to try and straighten out the many, many kinks.

'Yeah, about that,' he said. 'There's something I should tell you . . .'

Kat had felt a weight lift off her shoulders — for about ten seconds. The look on Jake's face brought that weight right back down with a thump.

'Tell me what?'

He squirmed uncomfortably.

'Nothing huge,' he assured her quickly. 'It's just that there's something you should know. Remember, ten years ago when you left, and we said we'd give it a year and see how we both felt?'

Of course she remembered. She had been eighteen, Jake twenty and they'd loved each other with all the passion their young lives could muster. Which was a lot. But they had also brought that passion to their arguments. Kat had nagged him constantly to leave the circus and he'd steadfastly refused, claiming life outside was no life at all.

'Of course I do.' She'd quickly realised her mistake and hadn't lasted anywhere near a year on the outside. But when she returned, Jake, who had claimed repeatedly he could never, ever leave, was gone — with no forwarding address.

'I came back at Christmas,' she said.

'I know. Delilah told me,' said Jake. 'But I didn't hear until the summer, when I returned like we'd arranged. I waited for you to come to the circus and find me, but you didn't.'

'You didn't look for me? Delilah had my address.'

'I did come looking for you,' he said. 'I saw you in a café with a group of friends. I followed you back to your house. It was brick, it had an upstairs and a little garden. Everything you'd always wanted.'

Her first house had been damp, draughty student accommodation with exactly the same boring view from the window every morning. She'd hated it.

'But why didn't you speak to me?'

'Because at Christmas you'd told everyone how great your life was and I could see with my own eyes that you were living your dream. What was the point in raking everything up again?'

'I only said that because I thought you'd moved on!' said Kat, aghast. She hadn't wanted her circus friends to pity her. And after all the things she'd said, she was too proud to come crawling back. Not without Jake. She thumped his arm.

'I can't believe this. We both came back at different times? Where had you been?'

'Anywhere that had an oil field and didn't ask too many questions.'

'You worked on an oil rig?'

'Yeah. I could climb, had great balance, a steady nerve and no fear of heights. They paid really well.'

She could imagine.

'But I don't get it. Why wouldn't you tell anyone what you were doing? Even Delilah didn't know where you were.'

'The places that paid best weren't big on health and safety. I couldn't risk it getting back to you.'

He was right; she'd have gone ballistic if she'd known he'd gone from one dangerous job to an even more dangerous one. But there was something she didn't understand.

'Why did you leave the circus at all? You always said it was the only life you wanted. That was why we couldn't be together.'

'Not all I ever wanted,' he said softly. 'It didn't take me long to realise that my life here was nothing without you. And since you didn't want to be here, I knew I would need money to support us while you were studying. I came back with enough to give us a start. But when I saw that I had already lost you, I returned to the rigs for a few more years.'

'Boy, have we made a mess of things,'

she said.

'Haven't we just.'

She rested her head on his shoulder and he put an arm around her. Kat felt his heartbeat, strong and maybe racing a little too fast with his emotions.

'So let me get this straight. You planned to show me how well you could cope in the outside world by taking the most high risk job you could find?'

'Actually I thought the deposit on a house might be the thing that convinced you.'

'Oh? Do you still have it? You know, I'm used to a pretty awesome standard of living now.'

She felt the rumble of laughter deep in his chest.

'It's all gone. When Delilah told me you were engaged, I blew it.'

He'd waited all that time? And then she knew.

'You bought the luxury caravan, didn't you?'

He nodded.

'You are so . . .' Words failed her.

'What?'

'Adorable. Stupid, but adorable. I could have married Nathan and become a gangster's moll and it would have been all your fault.'

'Gangster's moll would suit you.'

Their smiles slowly faded.

'So what now?' she asked. 'When this is over?'

His phone rang before he could answer.

'It's Nellie.'

Kat waited, reading his growing concern.

'We're on our way.'

'What is it?'

'Dmitri's been back for well over an hour. There's no sign of Noodle. Let's go.'

22

Nellie was waiting when they got back. Unfortunately so was Darrius. Kat had to contain her agitation and deal with the ringmaster first.

'Well?' asked Darrius eagerly.

'He's agreed,' she lied.

'Tell me.'

'There's nothing to tell. I'm supposed to contact him once the job is done and then he'll let us know the next steps.'

Darrius didn't like it.

'That wasn't the deal. How do I know you're telling the truth?'

'You know I met him. Finn followed me.'

'Just guarding my assets.'

'Well, you're the one who wanted to deal with the big boys, Darrius. This is how they work. They don't know you from Adam so they will only communicate via an intermediary. Me.'

He really didn't like it, but what could

he say?

'Just make sure you don't mess this up,' he snapped, and stormed off.

Kat hurried to where Jake, Nellie and the others had gathered.

'Dmitri came back two hours ago,' fretted Nellie. 'At first I wasn't too concerned — Noodle might have stopped for a bite to eat or the car might have broken down. But he would have called me by now, wouldn't he?'

'Have you rung him?'

She nodded. 'It went straight to voicemail.'

'Maybe he hasn't got a signal,' suggested Jake.

'Yes,' said Nellie. 'That's probably it.'

But none of them were convinced.

'Noodle has a good head on his shoulders,' said Kat, putting an arm around Nellie. 'He's not going to do anything stupid.'

'Do you really believe that?' asked Nellie with the tone of someone who had been bailing her husband out of trouble for years.

They both managed a smile, but there was no point in pretending.

'Kat, can you cover for Noodle in the show this afternoon?' asked Jake, drawing reproachful looks from everyone. 'Sorry. I'm sure he'll be back in time for this evening but we have to be practical.'

So Kat and Nellie did an old act where she dressed as a ballerina, and Nellie, complete with tutu and clown shoes, tried to copy her. It was unrehearsed and basic, but any slips were assumed to be part of the show and the kids loved it.

No one noticed Noodle's absence. Apart from Darrius. He grabbed Kat during the interval.

'Where's the clown?' he demanded.

'I thought you considered us all to be clowns?'

'Ha ha. The main clown. The funny one.'

Kat gave a deep bow.

'You know what I mean.'

'He has an upset tummy,' said Nellie. 'Not very pleasant for anyone around him, and mightily inconvenient in the ring.'

Darrius remained suspicious.

'Then he won't mind if I drop in and check on him,' he said.

'He wouldn't mind at all,' said Nellie sweetly. 'Though I suggest you don't wear those expensive boots of yours in case he throws up on them.'

Thankfully, Noodle turned up just before the evening show.

'Oh, merciful heavens!' Nellie threw herself into his arms.

'What?' Noodle looked baffled.

'We were worried sick about you,' scolded Nellie. 'You've been gone for hours.'

'Oh, yes, sorry,' said Noodle sheepishly. 'I took so many photos my phone battery died.'

'Photos of what?' asked Kat, her hopes rising.

Noodle's eyes shone. 'I've found her.'

* * *

His story had to wait until after the evening show but everyone's spirits were well and truly lifted as the news spread in a whisper.

Kat still had to replace Noodle in the evening performance as he stayed in his caravan and pretended to be ill in case anyone came looking. But as soon as was decently possible, a small crowd gathered in his caravan.

Noodle was grinning from ear to ear.

'So tell us,' demanded Kat.

'As you know, I was following Dmitri,' said Noodle. 'He went to the supermarket and got a bag of groceries and I assumed it would just be like all the other days. Especially as he went to a fast food place next. He never once looked behind him. Can you believe that?'

'Get to the point,' urged Jake.

'Well, to my surprise he didn't come back here but drove the other way and into the hills, which I found really promising. Eventually he turned down this track and I was even surer that I was on to something, but I couldn't follow — even a moron like Dmitri would have spotted me on that road. The sign at the end of the road said Cranmer Water Mill. It's only about half an hour away. I parked under the trees and walked. Luckily it wasn't far.

'There's a three-storey, stone-built building, a river, and a big pond with a lot of open grassland around it. I saw Dmitri knock at the door and a woman let him in. I've never seen her before.'

'Did you get close enough to see if Delilah was there?'

'No,' said Noodle. 'Not then. It was too open. Besides, even Dmitri would have recognised me if he'd seen me face to face.'

People murmured their disappointment.

'So how do you know Delilah was there?'

'I'm getting there,' said Noodle, the consummate performer. 'Dmitri stayed for over an hour. I would have phoned then, but I wanted to wait until I had something concrete. So I hung around, out of sight but close enough to see him leaving — I was worried he'd take Delilah with him and we'd lose her again. Anyway he did eventually leave — alone — so I was free to take a better look round.'

'Without the woman in the house seeing you?'

Noodle pulled a dog lead out of his pocket.

'I made sure she did see me. I also did a bit of calling for poor lost Mopsie.'

Mopsie had been the name of Delilah's dog when she was little.

'Get to the point,' said Jake.

'There were no cameras that I could see,' said Noodle. 'As I say, a stone building, three storeys. Few windows, quite small. Two big wooden doors, also pretty solid — they look as if they'd withstand a siege. There was a lot of construction equipment but I don't think it had been used in a while.'

Marty had his phone out. '*Cranmer Mill and Water Wheel*,' he read out. '*The mill and the water wheel are being restored to working order, though work is paused while they raise more funding.'*

'Sounds about right,' said Noodle.

'But Delilah!' urged Kat in growing exasperation.

'Patience.' Noodle too, took out his phone and showed them a series of snaps of the building along with a short video of a huge wooden wheel slowly being turned by a gently flowing stream. 'I don't think we can get in at any of the windows. However, there's this space.' He showed them a door-sized gap in the stone behind, and slightly above, the water wheel. 'I don't know if it should have a door, but it's currently wide open.'

Jake peered at the phone.

'You might be right. We'll have to go for a proper scout around before we make up our minds.'

'But *how do you know Delilah's there?*' Kat was ready to scream.

'Well I had to use a bit of subterfuge and excellent acting skills of course,' he said modestly.

'Noodle!' chorused half a dozen voices.

'I went back to the car for my accomplice.'

'But you went alone,' said Kat, puzzled.

'Did I?'

'Watch me,' called Captain and they all turned to look at the macaw. Seeing he had their attention he bobbed his head and did a little dance on the table, his claws clicking on the surface.

'I don't understand,' said Kat.

'Well, I went and knocked at the door, and asked the woman if she had seen my dog. She said no. I pulled the pathetic old man act.' In front of their eyes Noodle turned into an elderly gentleman, stooped and uncertain. 'Can you help me find my dog? Please? She's so little and doesn't keep well,' he said querulously. 'She refused again, quite rudely. I said, 'Is there anyone else here who can help me?' and she said —'

'Noodle, if you don't get to the point, I swear I will not be responsible for my actions,' warned Jake.

'Well, while I distracted her, Captain

here flew up to the windows.'

'And somehow he saw Delilah and came back and told you?' asked Marty sceptically.

'No, you daft bat. Delilah saw *him* and came to the window and I saw her.'

Captain started singing the old Tom Jones song.

'It's her,' said Noodle happily. 'We've found her.'

* * *

They talked long into the night. Noodle had a talent for 'casing a joint' as he put it and had taken a great many photos, until his phone died.

Everyone agreed the water wheel with the open doorway was the best way in. All someone had to do was ride the wheel on the upturn, jump into the building, find Delilah, free her and escape.

Jake, Xerxes and Delilah's brother Charlie were to be the rescue team. Jake and Charlie had the skills to get into the building, and Xerxes was muscle should it be needed. Kat insisted on being the driver because she couldn't bear to be left behind.

It was decided that the rescue should be the following night, after the show — a full day ahead of the planned robbery. Someone had been urgently despatched to the Mill to make sure Delilah wasn't spirited away while they were making their plans.

Once they had her safe, they could decide how to make sure Darrius got his just desserts.

* * *

Waking to heavy rain and full skies the next day didn't dampen anyone's spirits. Even those who didn't know the full details picked up on the mood and had a smile on their faces.

Kat came across Darrius studying Jake, Marty and Xerxes huddled together in the rain. Disbanding a few minutes later the men slapped each other on the back and went their separate ways with a jauntiness that had been missing of late.

Darrius glanced at Kat, then back at the men.

'What's going on? Has someone won the lottery?'

'People always get excited around pull down,' she suggested.

He raised an eyebrow and she had to think fast.

'They're finally getting on board with stealing the painting,' she improvised. 'I managed to convince them that the circus will benefit financially if we can pull this off and cover our tracks. That's going to be the tricky bit.' She looked him in the eye. 'If one of us goes down for this, our price increases, you do get that, don't you?'

'Yes, yes,' he said.

'I mean it.' She pressed her point, hoping to distract him. 'If someone gets arrested then you're paying for their silence.'

Darrius understood money. She hoped she had convinced him.

Apparently not. He finally gave her

his full attention, his grey eyes glittering coldly.

'I hear what you are saying, but perhaps you should gather the Scooby gang, Ms Turnado.'

'Why?' Her heart fluttered in a rising panic she fought to hide. All they needed was twelve hours. After tonight, Delilah would be free.

'Their excitement is contagious,' said Darrius. 'I've decided to bring the robbery forward. We'll do it tonight.'

23

'What tipped him off?' demanded Jake. They were gathered glumly in his caravan after the afternoon show, the rain drumming on the roof.

'We were just too cheerful,' said Noodle, glumly. 'He didn't like it.'

Not only had Darrius decided to bring the robbery forward, he had decreed that Jake, Kat and Xerxes should be the ones to carry it out. No arguments were allowed. It was as if he knew something was up and wanted to keep them close. Kat had to wonder if they had underestimated his intelligence.

'We can still do it,' said Charlie. 'If you three are in the show, then Marty and I —'

Jake shook his head.

'Darrius will notice if anyone is missing. And if he gets any more suspicious, he just has to make a call and we might never find Delilah.'

'After the show then,' said Charlie, desperately.

'Again, that's no use. The robbery should be in progress then and it will be touch and go whether any of us can get to the mill and free her before the others have to hand over the painting. Plus, in theory, Darrius should have brought her here at gunpoint by then. There's too big a risk of something going wrong or someone getting hurt. It has to be during the show, before the robbery.'

Kat could see the lines of strain on his face. and knew how he felt. To be this close to their goal, and then be thwarted, was the worst feeling ever.

'Maybe there's a way,' she said tentatively.

Everyone looked at her.

'How?' asked Marty.

'He wants the painting stolen tonight after the show. Anyone who has any chance of rescuing Delilah will be in the show. Darrius is making a point of keeping us all close.'

'We get that. So?'

'So what if we can convince him we are close?' She outlined her plan.

Jake pondered. 'It might work.' And then, with much more confidence, 'Actually, it might work!'

* * *

They had learned their lesson and were careful to keep their renewed hope hidden as they prepared for the evening show. The incessant rain and churning mud certainly dampened the mood.

Jake had to change the order of some acts for the plan to work, but that wasn't unusual. They had been over the plan and over it again. Everyone had their job and knew what to do.

Late afternoon, Noodle had taken a car and hidden it under trees about a hundred yards from the gates of Huntersly Hall.

Nellie slipped an extra special blend of spices into the burger she served to Finn and Dmitri at tea time. Yes, they could taste the heat, but Nellie's cheery 'Hope it's not too hot for you, boys' had challenged their manhood and ensured they would eat every last bit, even when their eyes were streaming. Hopefully they would want to stay close to a bathroom and therefore be out of commission for the rest of the evening.

Jake did his usual trapeze act in the first half, then the aerial silk act with Ivanna. As soon as he was done he changed into his skeleton costume for the Wheel of Death, which would be the closing act of the evening. He went around barking orders at people, making himself highly visible.

Kat did her knife-throwing act with Xerxes then changed into jeans and a very gaudy top, her long pony tail swinging beneath a peaked baseball cap as she set up the hot dog stand.

Darrius made some comment about her T-shirt and Jake saw her snap back at him.

Perfect. If she had been nice at this stage Darrius would have wondered what was going on. But Jake suspected Kat hadn't had to fake her nervous tension. Everyone was looking a bit strained, even those with little idea what was afoot.

Only Darrius seemed unaffected. In fact he appeared flushed with excitement.

At a preordained point in the evening, Jake whispered to Ivanna, who nodded and slipped behind a dressing screen. That was Kat's cue to join her. A few minutes later, Ivanna emerged wearing Kat's loud T-shirt and baseball cap, her long dark hair in a high ponytail. She went straight to serving hot dogs while Kat, now dressed in body-hugging black from head to toe, sneaked out of the tent.

Jake caught Charlie's eye, and soon they too were behind a screen, swapping clothes. Charlie donned the skeleton outfit while Jake wore unrelieved black.

'Stay where Darrius can see you,' he told Charlie '— but not so close that he sees you're not me.'

'Relax,' said Charlie. 'We got this. Xerxes is stuck to him like glue. Apparently the big man is really nervous about tonight. He's driving Darrius up the wall with all his questions.'

Now it was Jake's turn to sneak away. Charlie and Ivanna could pass for him and Kat at a distance. And the others were more than capable of ensuring Darrius was kept at that distance.

Kat was waiting at the back of the tent, mounted on a black horse and holding the reins of a second. The rain continued to tip down and she was already soaked. Jake leaped onto his horse. With a touch of their heels, and riding bareback, they raced in the direction of the road. Reaching the wall, they leaped off, sending the horses home with a slap on the rump.

Avoiding the gate, they scaled the wall and ran to where Noodle had left the car. Only once they were inside the car did they breathe.

'This is going to work.' said Kat and Jake wasn't sure which one of them she was trying to convince.

He nodded grimly.

The mill was thirty minutes away, so

sneaking out half way through the show would buy valuable time. With luck they could be there and back with Delilah even before the end of the show. In the meantime, Charlie and Ivanna would keep one step away from Darrius, so that hopefully he would never notice the substitution. When he came looking for them at the end of the show, Xerxes would tell him that they were already at the stable block, getting ready to scale the drainpipe. They were counting on the fact that Darrius wouldn't want to get too close to the action, just in case something went wrong.

Kat reached for his hand.

'It feels good to be finally doing something, doesn't it?'

He knew exactly what she meant; adrenalin was coursing through him too.

* * *

The filthy weather had the benefit of keeping people at home so they made up even more time on the road. Jake took a few precious extra seconds to park the car ready for a quick getaway.

As they got out, the rain was still coming down hard. That would make things more difficult, but Jake was feeling more confident by the minute.

'This way,' he told Kat and they set off.

The waterlogged ground sucked at their feet but the mill was just ahead, a shadow on the skyline. Jake was aware that with all the rain, the river was running way faster than when Noodle had filmed it, but he prayed it wouldn't interfere with their plans.

Then he slipped on the wet grass and fell. Badly.

Kat was several yards in front before she noticed. She immediately retraced her steps.

'What happened? Are you OK?'

'My ankle.' Jake's voice grated with pain.

'Is it broken?' Kat didn't try to hide her fear.

He shook his head. 'No. I just need

a minute.'

He sat on the soggy grass, while the rain continued to fall. Kat sat on her heels, studying his face. Whatever he said, his ankle was bad.

'Can you stand?'

He nodded and lurched to his feet, struggling to put any weight on the injured foot. She saw him look desperately towards the building.

'I'll be fine,' he said. 'I just have to get on the wheel and let it lift me up.'

'And how will you get off it at the top?' she asked practically. 'If you can barely stand, how will you jump? If your ankle gives way on landing, we'll have two people trapped inside instead of one.'

She didn't even mention that if he missed his timing or footing, the wheel would drag him down into the dark, churning water.

'I can do it —'

'No.' She stood up. 'You can't. It's too risky.'

'But —'

'Didn't you always tell me life was a

calculated risk? How are your calculations working out?'

'I could ring Marty,' said Jake, white-faced.

'No time.' She looked at the water wheel, turning faster by the minute. 'It has to be me.'

'No!'

'It's the only way,' she said, dry-mouthed. 'I'm not leaving here without her.'

She knew he knew she was right.

'Just get in, open the door and I'll do the rest,' he begged.

'No. I'll stick to the plan.' She kissed him, quick and hard on the lips. 'This shouldn't take long. Try to get under some shelter.' Then she ran towards the mill before she lost her nerve.

Kat's heart pounded as she stood before the massive wooden wheel. Noodle's photos yesterday had shown how a part of the river had been diverted to turn the wheel. There was a sluice gate that could be raised or lowered to control the flow of water passing over the paddles of the wheel. At the current river speed, Kat had no chance of working the sluice. Even Xerxes would have struggled.

She stood, mesmerised by the wheel, which this close, was a dripping, fast-spinning monster. There, above it, was the shadowy door-like opening. Maybe a grain loft or something to do with the mill's grinding wheels. That doorway was Kat's target.

All she had to do was get on the wheel, let it lift her and jump at exactly the right moment.

Right.

Fear almost paralysed her. But Delilah was in there somewhere, waiting to be rescued. They couldn't come this far only to leave without her.

She watched the wheel for a few rotations then, her heart in her mouth, took an almighty leap.

Her hands caught first, then her feet found purchase. Water sprayed in her face and she was spluttering, scrabbling and the wheel was lifting her and her face was clear of the water and she had to jump, would only have this one chance . . .

The wheel reached its zenith; any second now it would start its plunging, roaring, descent.

And suddenly Kat's fear was gone, replaced by instinct and laser-like focus. She could do this. She really could.

Her leg muscles bunched as she chose her moment, then launched into the air.

Spray splashed on her face, filling her mouth, almost blinding her. But the doorway was there. Her knee scraped stone, more stone clipped her ankle, buffeting her and she adjusted, twisting her body in mid-air. Suddenly she was out of the rain, crashing down onto a hard surface. She was in!

Landing heavily, she lay on her back on bare wood, trying to collect herself. She'd swallowed a lot of water but didn't dare cough.

But she had done the seemingly impossible. She had faced her biggest nightmare — her very own Wheel of

Death — and survived using skill and judgement.

She had faced her fear; and it felt incredible.

24

Kat allowed herself a few minutes, then rose to her feet. A TV was playing downstairs, the volume turned up against the sound of rushing water, but she could hear no other noise.

Noodle had reported seeing Delilah at a third floor window. Kat inched around a pair of huge millstones, then along a narrow corridor, her feet squelching and leaving a trail of wet footprints. She'd better rescue Delilah before anyone came to check on their prisoner.

There were signs of renovation on the third floor but only one room had a door. Kat put her ear to it. Nothing. Except . . . was that the faint rattle of a chain?

'Delilah?' she whispered urgently. The rattling stopped. 'Del, it's me.'

'Kat?' There was surprise, joy, fear, so many emotions in that one word. 'Get me out of here.'

'Two minutes.' Kat had her lock picks tucked into her bra, where they were still snug and secure. It took more like five minutes — she was out of practice — before she pushed the door open. New, it swung easily, and more to the point, silently.

Delilah sat cross-legged on a low futon. One ankle was attached to a chain fastened to the floor, which would have allowed her to walk in a circle of perhaps five feet. Just enough to see out of the window if she craned her neck. Her hands were bound behind her.

'It *is* you,' said Delilah in shock. 'Get me out of these.' She half turned, showing the handcuffs.

Rage surged through Kat, but she tamped it down. Moments later Delilah was hugging her.

'I can't believe it,' she babbled, over and over. 'I mean I knew someone would come but it was so long . . . Euww. You're soaking wet. Oh, I can't believe it. Thank you!'

Kat returned her joyful hug but had

to prise her off so she could work on the lock of the ankle chain.

'We have to get out of here. You can tell me everything once we're safely in the car.'

Delilah nodded, and Kat was furious at seeing the fear in her friend's eyes; Delilah, who was scared of nothing.

'How many of them are there?' asked Kat.

'Just one. Brenda.' Delilah spat the name. 'She must have been a prison guard in hell in a previous life. She's married to that slob, Dmitri.' She rubbed her ankle and saw Kat looking at the chafe marks. 'They used rope at first but I got out of that easily. Then they brought the handcuffs but I keep a tiny pick in my shoes so they were easy to get out of, too. Until they took the pick, and my shoes and then added the ankle chain for good measure. I tried to escape. I really did. I mean, I—'

'Shhh,' said Kat. Delilah hadn't had anyone to speak to for a week and she always did have a lot to say. 'Tell me later.'

Delilah nodded, tears spilling over.

'Who else is here?'

'Jake.'

'Jake? Is that it? I expected the cavalry!'

'Long story, but horses were involved if that makes you feel better. And a parrot.'

Delilah smiled her old smile. 'Captain. I saw him. He's getting a whole sack of brazil nuts from me.'

'Come on.'

They tiptoed downstairs. There was a small room to the right of a door that once probably led to the miller's office. The TV sounds came from there.

The door was double bolted and they gently slipped the bolts free. But when they tried to open it, it wouldn't budge.

Locked. And there was no key.

Kat and Delilah looked at each other, then crept towards the office. They saw a small kitchen area with a kettle and a hotplate. A rather large woman was sprawled on a shabby sofa in front of the TV.

Kat spotted a heavy iron key on a hook on the wall at the other side of the office door and pointed it out to Delilah, who nodded. Kat indicated that she would circle round and approach it from the other side. Delilah gestured that no, she would get it and Kat should stay put. A brief, silent argument ensued but before a decision could be reached a phone rang, jolting them both to stillness.

Brenda muted the TV and answered.

'Hello?' She listened. 'Can't Dmitri come and get her? But it's raining.' She sighed. 'OK, OK. But I'm keeping her shoes. Yeah. I'll be about an hour. I told you, it's raining! The roads will be mud and I've still got to get her out of the house and into the car. Proper uncooperative, she is.'

Brenda stood up and her cigarette fell from her lip in shock when she saw Kat standing there.

Kat looked around for a weapon. Brenda was twice her size but if they had to fight it out, so be it.

There was a whooshing noise; Brenda

dropped like a stone. Delilah stood behind, holding a pan.

'I thought you were getting the key?' she said sweetly.

Kat grinned, seized the key and rammed it into the lock. Pulling the door open, she just managed to duck as Jake swung a tree branch at her. He blinked and managed to avert the blow.

'Thank God,' he said, dropping the weapon so he could pull Kat against him.

'Hey, I'm the one being rescued,' said Delilah.

'You didn't see what she did,' said Jake. 'I swear my whole life passed before my eyes. You were incredible. Don't ever put me through that again,' he told Kat almost squeezing the life out of her.

'Through what?' she asked.

'I thought you were going to die!'

'It was a calculated risk,' she protested.

'We'll talk about that later,' said Jake grimly.

Delilah had been following all this with interest. Now a grin lit up her face.

'So it's like that, is it? About time is all I can say.' While she spoke, she yanked a pair of bright pink trainers off Brenda's feet.

The shoes were lumpy and misshapen. Like the bare feet.

Kat wrinkled her nose. 'Surely you're not going to wear those?'

Delilah grimaced as she gingerly carried the shoes to the door and threw them as far as she could into the rainy night. 'Never disrespect my shoes,' she told the still unconscious Brenda, then turned to Jake and opened her arms for a hug. 'Is it my turn now?'

* * *

'So what happened after we left?' asked Jake. They were in his caravan. Kat was sitting on his knee since there were no seats left.

It seemed like half the circus had crammed themselves in. Kat and Delilah were fresh from the shower, wrapped in cosy blankets and drinking Nellie's special hot chocolate. Delilah had refused point blank to go back to her own caravan until it had been fumigated.

'Well, while we were waiting for you or Kat to call, we stuck to the plan,' said Charlie. 'We kept out of Darrius' way while the show was on. Of course at the end he came looking for us but Xerxes here told him we were already up by the stable block, getting ready. As hoped, Darrius kept his distance. We stalled a bit, pretending to wait for the rain to stop. Then, when we finally got the call, we turned on him. Finn and Dmitri were still incapacitated so he wasn't feeling quite so cocky. Especially as Noodle had pinched his gun and replaced it with one that fired confetti.'

'But you let him go!' protested Delilah. 'That seems so unfair!'

'We-e-elll,' drawled Marty. 'About that.'

'What?'

'While everyone was keeping Darrius distracted, I might have nipped up the drainpipe and stolen the painting. Good plan by the way, Kat. It worked perfectly.'

'You did what?' She almost fell off Jake's knee, giving him an excuse to grip her more tightly. In fact he might never let her go again.

'I stole the painting,' repeated Marty. 'They'll discover it's missing come morning. Then, Kat, you could call your friend Paul and possibly have him track down Darrius and check the boot of his car.'

Her jaw dropped.

'You planted the painting on him?'

Marty nodded cheerfully. 'It was Jake's idea. It seemed a shame that Darrius should get off scot free after all he put us through.'

For a second there was total silence in the caravan, then it rocked with laughter.

Jake sighed happily, all once more right with his world. Delilah was safe. Kat was in his arms.

And the circus had protected its own.

25

Three days later Kat and Jake were walking on the beach near their new pitch.

'I can't believe how light I feel,' said Jake skimming a stone.

'Me neither. It's as if a load has been lifted.'

'Many, many loads. So your suspension is truly over?' he asked.

She nodded. 'Completely exonerated. And I finally told Paul about the necklace. He reckons that since the investigation missed it completely, I should just keep quiet about it. Now Nathan has done a deal, he has just as much to lose as I do so I doubt he'll mention it to anyone. I'm supposed to report for duty on Monday.'

'Supposed to?' She could almost see Jake's ears prick up.

'Yeah.' She sat down on the warm sand.

He joined her. 'Watching you prepare

to ride that water wheel was the worst moment of my life,' he said quietly. 'I mean, I know circus work looks dangerous but I work really hard to minimise the risks, no matter how it seems to the audience, I make sure everyone is properly trained for the task in hand, and stays within their capabilities. It's the only way I can sleep at night. What you did . . . my heart was in my mouth.'

'What I did was clearly within my capabilities,' she pointed out.

'I know. But I love you, Kat. I think what I'm trying to say is that I finally understand what you went through, watching me on The Wheel night after night. I couldn't bear to see you taking those kinds of risks every day. I'll actually rest easier knowing that you're back in law enforcement.'

'You do know that rescuing kidnap victims is usually more of a police than a circus matter, don't you?' she teased.

'You know what I mean,' he said. 'The police have rules. Your Paul would never have allowed you to pull that kind of stunt.'

'No. But if we'd followed the rules, who knows what might have happened to Delilah?' she said seriously.

Should she tell him about the sheer adrenalin rush of the rescue? Of the feeling of pushing herself to the limits and winning against the odds? He of all people would surely understand that kind of thrill. After all, he'd spent years trying to explain it to her.

'I'd do it again in a heartbeat,' she said.

'That's what I'm worried about.'

'No, listen,' she said eagerly. 'I love being a detective. But sometimes the constraints are . . . frustrating. We don't always get the job done. Whereas in the circus . . .'

'We do what it takes.'

'Exactly.'

'So what are you saying?'

'That while it's nice that the police will have me back, I'm not sure that I want to go.'

'What do you plan to do instead?'

He wasn't looking at her, just staring

out over the waves.

She elbowed him in the ribs.

'Well, I thought I could stay here. I thought you wanted me here?'

Her heart was hammering. Had she misread this entirely?

'It might be possible,' said Jake slowly. 'You'd have to just work the concessions. The goats maybe. I could get some turtle doves and you could devise a nice act with them . . .'

Was he serious? No. She saw his jaw twitch; he was trying so hard not to laugh.

'You really had me going there!' Kat lay back on the sand and pulled him down with her for a kiss. 'You're lucky I don't push you right into the sea!' She looked up into his twinkling green eyes. 'Anyway, I'm not leaving. Circus is in my blood, remember. Besides, if Nathan ever did choose to reveal those photos, I'd be back in hot water and maybe not so lucky the next time.'

She saw colour rush over Jake's cheeks.

'About that . . .'

'What? What have you done?'

He slid a packet of photos out of his pocket and handed them to her. She leafed through them in disbelief.

'How did you get these? The police searched . . .'

'They did, but they didn't have Noodle. I wouldn't want to have to hide anything from that man.'

'You broke into Nathan's house?'

'You just said it. The circus takes care of its own.' His expression turned serious. 'Are you one of ours, Kat Turnado? Is that what you are saying?'

'I'm yours,' she agreed, wrapping her arms around his neck. 'Now and forever.'

And she pulled him into her arms for a long, lingering kiss that truly felt like home.